THE LOST
BROTHER

Taniquelle Tulipano

A *Bella Tulip* Book
First published in the United Kingdom by CreateSpace 2015
This edition is published by Bella Tulip Publishing 2016

THE LOST BROTHER

Paperback 9780993562631
Kindle 9780993562648
ePub 9780993562655

Editing/Proofreading Rebecca Weeks, Rebecca's editing services

Book formatted by Taniquelle Tulipano

Bella Tulip Publishing
83 Ducie Street
Manchester
M1 2JQ

www.bellatulippublishing.com

My love for you knows no bounds.
This is for you B.

PROLOGUE

If you had told me two months ago what fate had planned for these last eight weeks, I would have laughed at you. I would have wondered how you had been discharged from the theoretical mental asylum I got you put in! You see, three months ago, my life was perfect; everything was as it should be. For the very first time in my life, I was in love and content. It wasn't a conventional love, but I was happy. Don't get me wrong, I missed my previous life and the people in it, but I was living a new life, the life I was meant to lead. I was no longer a naive little girl. I had grown into a mature woman with a deeper understanding of the world around her. It never occurred to me that things could go wrong, but that was exactly what happened. My perfect dream life was ripped away from me, but as awful as it was, it now pales in comparison to the here and now. Now, my orchestra is dead, my hopes and dreams are smashed, and my life is broken. I need a miracle, and I need it fast … before it's too late.

CHAPTER ONE

Rosannah

I always thought that the worst day of my entire life would somehow involve my mother. How terrible does that sound? It's sad, but it goes without saying that she's a nightmare. She has dictated how I should live my life and has meddled incessantly in things she shouldn't.

Well, it turns out I was wrong. It was not my mother but two male vampires who gave me the worst day of my life—Raphael, the drop-dead gorgeous hunk, and Nicholas, one of his cheeky younger twin brothers. Raphael's home had become a prison for me since I *discovered* he was a vampire. Neither he nor any other vampire that tried could brainwash me to forget what they were. I was a liability to them, but over time, feelings developed between Raphael and me, and a strange yet comfortable relationship started between us. How did it go so terribly wrong? I don't know entirely. All I do know is that Raphael and Nicholas had an argument. I only caught the tail end of it, but it wasn't enough for me to figure out what it was all about. Whatever the problem was, it resulted in Raphael ordering me out of his home.

That fateful day was four weeks ago. A lot has changed since then, including me questioning my sanity. I decided I needed to throw myself back into work. After what had happened with Raphael and his vampire friends and family, I needed normality in my life again—something I could grab with my two bare hands and never let go. I wanted to wrap myself up in that suffocating cotton wool and forget that Raphael and vampires existed. Pretend that my heart wasn't shattered into a million different pieces.

The day after I got home from Raphael's should have been a normal day. I should have met Brianna, driven us to work, and explained that the *holiday* they were brainwashed into thinking I was on was cut short. Something very bizarre unfolded instead.

The first sign that something strange was going on started early that morning with a horn sounding outside. Out of curiosity, I looked out of my front room window and saw an unknown car sat at the curb. That in and of itself was not unusual. What was out of the ordinary was seeing Brianna dash out of our apartment and jumping into it. I tried to see who was driving, but from my viewpoint, it was practically impossible. Racing through my apartment, I got ready for work, and just before I left, I looked at my answering machine. It was still full because I hadn't been able to face all of my mother's messages. She was probably having kittens not knowing why I hadn't returned any of her calls. It was funny; you'd think that if she were that worried, then she would have visited. How did I know she hadn't visited? She always made a point of sticking a rather rude and blunt note through the door when she'd come over unannounced and I hadn't been in. There was no note amongst my surprisingly small pile of mail. I made a mental note to delete all the messages later that day and dashed out. I jumped into Anthea and turned her on. "This Charming Man" by The Smiths was playing; a much-loved song that I had a habit of screaming the lyrics.

The journey was short and sweet, but my nerves played at me. I couldn't shake the image of Brianna jumping into that car. Who could be giving her a lift? I couldn't think of anyone. I was also worried about the questions I'd get when I would tell work that I missed home so much that I'd cut my *holiday* short.

After I had parked up, I headed into the office. It had only been a couple of weeks since I had been there, but I still felt out of sorts.

Brianna and Marie were talking as I entered and paused to give me a warm and welcoming smile. Fortunately, Paul wasn't in yet.

"I know I should have called to say I was cutting my holiday short but an enormous brown eye' I'm here now," I said as I approached them, forcing a smile.

"What holiday?" Brianna laughed.

"I have been away for two weeks, haven't I?" I asked, slightly confused.

"We saw you yesterday, but if it means that much, we've missed you, too." Marie chuckled.

"But I'm sure I've been away," I insisted.

"Rosannah, you're so funny. You haven't been away at all. Isn't that right?" Brianna asked Paul, who had just walked in.

"If you hadn't been in, I'd know," he said, looking at me questioningly. I was extremely confused. What the hell had happened? I was pretty sure that I had been taken hostage by a vampire who was quite literally sex on legs, but all of my work colleagues were adamant that I hadn't been anywhere.

For most of that morning, I worked in a stunned silence, only speaking when I had to.

As if that morning wasn't bad enough, there was more to come. Brianna dragged me to the cafe for lunch like we normally do. Mike came wandering over to us once we had sat down in our usual spot.

"Hello, ladies." Mike smiled.

"When was the last time I was here, Mike?" I blurted out to him. His smile dropped into confusion.

"Well, yesterday, Rosannah," he said, worry crossing his wrinkled face. Thinking quickly, I forced a smile.

"I love it here so much I come here every day," I said hunching up my shoulders. A smile restored itself on his face.

"That's great to hear. And yes, you certainly do come here every day," he said shooting Brianna a questioning look. So even Mike was sure I hadn't been away, too. "The usual?" he asked.

"Yes." Brianna grinned, and Mike wandered back off to the kitchen. Was everything that had happened with Raphael a dream? It couldn't have been. I knew that Brianna and Marie had met Raphael. I had seen it happen, hadn't I? I decided the next plan of action was to ask her about him.

"So what did you think of Raphael?" I asked quietly.

"Who's that?" she asked scrunching up her face.

"You know, Raphael Monstrum. The Monstrum place," I asked incredulously.

"I've never met him and never will by the looks of it. The valuation fell through. It's a crying shame. Surely you remember? Maybe not. It makes no difference to you. I, on the other hand, am still pretty gutted. I was so close to finding out what lies behind that front door, and now I'll never know." She sighed. No valuation? What was she talking about? *I* had done the valuation! Well, questionnaire! Maybe she was lying, but why would she? And that didn't explain Marie, Paul, *and* Mike saying the same thing, too.

I had one thing left to check and confirm my possible madness. I needed to see the files back at the office. Once our lunch arrived, I ate as quickly as I could, without it looking too suspect, and dragged Brianna back to work.

I raced into Marie's office, making her jump in the process. "I'm sorry, Marie." I smiled apologetically. "Would it be possible if I could look at the Monstrum file?" I asked.

"Yes, certainly; it's over there in the filing cabinet." She smiled. I had been in this cabinet many times before without giving it much thought, but this time, my head was crammed with worry and anxiety about what I would find in it that particular time. I opened the drawer that housed M and sifted through the files. Among many names, I remembered sat the Monstrum one. With shaky and sweaty hands, I plucked it from its hanging folder and opened it. Across the first and the only page was the word *finished* stamped on it. At the bottom of the page, *no longer wishes to have house evaluated* was scrawled in *my* handwriting. The piece of paper was the enquiry sheet that Marie had filled out. I looked in the hanging file just to make sure nothing had fallen out. Nothing else was there but the other files. My questionnaire was gone.

"Everything okay?" asked Marie.

"Oh. Yes. Fine. Everything is. Fine," I said with a forced a smile. I returned the file and walked in a zombie state back to my chair.

I was incredibly thankful that no one walked in or even called my phone for the rest of the day as I wasn't able to say much.

The craziness didn't stop there because that day hadn't been insane enough, right? When I got home after work, all the messages on my answer machine were gone apart from the normal one from my mother today. *I could have sworn it was full that morning when I left for work!*

I had the usual telephone conversation I have with my mother, who didn't mention anything out of the ordinary. I was faced with something quite perplexing. On the one hand, I had my memories that told me I had discovered a client, Raphael, was a vampire and said discovery led him to hold me captive for roughly two weeks. I had fallen head over heels in love with Raphael and had my heart broken and thrown out of his home in a matter of nearly fourteen days. On the other hand, I had my work colleagues, Mike, and the Monstrum file telling me that none of my memories had actually happened. I have found it too difficult to think of my time with the vampires as make-believe because there is one piece of evidence that is contrary to the rest, my virginity. Later, on that fateful day after I had put the phone down to my mother, I had a shower. For the first time in my life, I inserted a finger into myself followed by another. My virginity was gone. If everything that had happened with Raphael wasn't real, then what the hell happened to me?

I phoned Brianna and got her to come up to mine. According to her,I took her to and from work every day except that morning when she had left early and gotten a lift. She said every night I stayed in, and no one came up. She would know because my flat is the only one above her mum's. The information clashed painfully against knowing that I had lost my virginity.

I have since stopped asking Brianna about the time I was away because she's beginning to get concerned. I have vaguely filed it somewhere in my brain. I just have to forget about it.

CHAPTER TWO

Rosannah

For the past four weeks, the craziness hasn't just been limited to vampires and work. Brianna has gotten herself a boyfriend, Michael. He's the lift-giver from *that* morning. It's not the fact that she has a boyfriend that I find strange. It's the fact I haven't met him yet. All Brianna has talked about is Michael. She gushed about how gorgeous he is and how incredible he is in the bedroom. According to her, I need to meet him, but this has yet to materialize.

Brianna and Michael have spent the last week in Wales, and she is expected back today. I have been eagerly awaiting Brianna's return since I got up this morning. She was due back at 9am, and it's now late afternoon. Every time a car has pulled up outside, I've dashed to the window only to be disappointed. The day has seriously dragged on like this, and my patience has worn thin. Through exasperation, I decide that the next car is the last one I'll dash to the window for. I don't have to wait long. This time, a cab pulls up, and a very slim redhead gets out. I can't see their face, but I know it's not Brianna. I resign myself back to the couch and flop down with a large huff. Marmalade jumps up and snuggles on my lap. Stroking her with one hand, I use the other to press play on my Sky remote. Instantly, Southern Rockhopper Penguins are carrying on their assault over rocks and boulders on the screen. They are the cutest little things and always make me think of

Lovelace from *Happy Feet*. It's really not hard to do if you've seen the film.

Ring. The doorbell sounds and Marmalade jumps, her back arched up. Who could it possibly be? It can't be Brianna because I haven't seen her arrive, and I can tell by the ring that it's not my mother, thank goodness. Marmalade hops off my lap, and I pause the TV. I feel annoyed that it's not my best friend. Not only do I want to hear everything about Brianna's holiday, but I've also missed her terribly.

I've also had to contend with Paul virtually all on my own. Marie went out doing all of the valuations while Paul and I stayed in the office taking calls. I didn't think Paul could get anymore rude and obnoxious, but I have to say, Paul really did outdo himself.

I wander over to the door and look through the spy hole. A huge brown eye fills my view. I can barely contain my curiosity as I unlock and open the door. All I see is bright red hair and a huge grin as the lady at my door throws herself at me, pulling me into a tight hug. I stand here for a minute wondering who the hell this is. Who gives a huge hug to someone they don't know? I pat her on the back, and she squeals in my ear. She's happy to see me. Pulling back, I take in her appearance. It's the redhead from the cab earlier. She looks familiar but so different at the same time.

"It's me. Brianna." She grins. I look at her for a minute. "You know, your best friend? Surely you haven't already forgotten me!" She laughs. I see her eyes shine with amusement, and it dawns on me.

"Oh, my God," I mumble as I stand and stare at her. She's lost *so* much weight and her once light brown frizzy hair is now bright red and polka straight. She looks like a completely different person.

"You can put your tongue away now," she jokes.

"Wow, you look incredible," I manage.

"Aren't you going to invite me in?" she asks with a giggle.

"Oh yeah, sure. Come in," I say moving out of the way. I wait until she enters, and then I close the front door. "Would you like some tea?" I ask her.

"No sugar or milk please," she practically sings at me as she goes to sits down. Whoa, what's happened to my best friend? This girl usually mixed six, yes six, teaspoons of sugar in her extremely milky tea.

I make our tea almost in a daze and sit down next to her. Shaking my head, I clear my thoughts to stop anything stupid spilling from my lips. "How was the holiday?" I ask, blowing into my cup. I smile in relief that my brain to mouth filter has worked. Thankfully, Brianna doesn't appear to notice.

"It was amazing! It was one of those workout holidays, and to top it off, I got a full body workout from Michael. Every night, all night. That man is a machine!" she exclaims. I smile, remembering when I called Evangeline one. I will file that away in my crazy-ass thoughts safe.

Brianna proceeds to tell me all the ins and outs of her holiday, or should I say all of *her* ins and outs with Michael. Another surprise, to add to all the other ones, is that she sounds like she's completely in love with him. I feel jealous that she has her man, but I don't have mine. Another thought to lock away.

17

"You don't look as shocked about my sexual antics as you usually do," Brianna says with surprise. I know it's been a while since she has told me anything remotely explicit, but it doesn't seem to faze me anymore. I stop my thoughts before they run down a path I don't want them to go.

"Maybe I've gotten used to hearing about them." I shrug.

"Maybe." She grins and gets up. I follow suit. "I'd really like you to meet Michael," she says as we reach the door. The first time she said this to me, I could barely contain my joy, but this is possibly the millionth time she's said this to me. The element of excitement has been doused by broken promises. "He's been so busy, but now he can meet you. Are you free this evening? Tout C'est Magnifique?" she asks. Wow, could this finally happen? I'll believe it when I see it. Michael or no Michael, at least, Brianna and I will eat at our favourite restaurant tonight. Located just minutes from where we live, they cook the most amazing French food there.

"Yes!" I half laugh, half yell.

"You really want to meet him huh?" She giggles.

"I've been dying to meet him," I say exasperated.

"Meet us at the restaurant. We have a reservation for eight pm." She smiles as she opens the door and leaves. I close and lock the door behind her and rush to the bathroom for a shower.

While I'm washing, my mind starts racing. Something doesn't quite make sense. Brianna has gone on nonstop about how great Michael is and how I need to meet him. It never got further than her simply saying it, but now she's come back from holiday, looking remarkably different, and she has already made a reservation for me to meet him. It's a very popular place with a waiting list. He would have had to make the reservation a few days ago before she even got home. Something isn't quite right about all of this, but I put the uneasy feeling aside because I might be finally meeting the elusive Michael.

By the time I'm ready, it's 7:45 pm. The amount of notice Brianna gave me wasn't much, and I run downstairs, power walking my way to Tout C'est Magnifique. I'm so excited to be eating there when I meet Michael for the first time. It's very fitting to meet the guy who's completely captured my best friend's heart at our favourite place to visit. I'm there within ten minutes and see Brianna waving at me when I enter. I manage to dodge the host, and I make my way over to Brianna's table. She stands to introduce Michael. A strong looking man with his back to me stands up and turns to face me with a smile. As soon as I see his face, my heart starts to pound. My palms get clammy, and I can hardly breathe.

"Rosannah, are you okay? You've gone as white as a sheet," Brianna asks, concerned. I ignore her and continue to stare at the man whose face I would recognise anywhere. I'm staring into the face of Nicholas, one of the cheeky vampire twin brothers of Raphael, the client I supposedly never met. The last time I saw them comes flooding into my brain like a tidal wave.

I had come down the stairs of Raphael's house because I'd heard a commotion and I'd wanted to see what was going on. Raphael and Nicholas had been arguing in the kitchen doorway about something I couldn't figure out, and Lawrence and Evangeline were there, too. As I approached them all, Nicholas pushed Raphael so hard that he flew backwards and smashed through his monster of a front door. I remember just how terrifying Nicholas had looked. He was furious, and thank goodness, Lawrence and Evangeline held him back. Raphael made his way back to Nicholas and tried to calm him down. Then Raphael ordered me out of his home. Pain stabs at my stomach. I had put all of this to rest. Well, I tried best I could and now here stands proof of my two weeks in the Monstrum residence.

Nicholas's brow furrows slightly with concern, but there's not even the slightest flicker of recognition.

"Nicholas," I manage to blurt out. His face instantly scrunches up.

"It's Michael," he says, clearly insulted. I don't say anything and continue to assess him. He looks just like Nicholas, and he even sounds like him! The only difference between Nicholas and the guy stood in front of me is his dark hair is cut very short, and his eyes are a rich chocolate brown. His skin even has some colour to it.

"Rosannah, why don't you sit down and I'll get you a drink. You look like you need it," exclaims Brianna as she sits back down. I slide in next to her and face *Michael*.

All through the evening, I watch every move Michael makes as sneakily as I can. If he is Nicholas, he's doing a damn good job of pretending he's not. I even asked him a barrage of questions about his history. He never missed a beat, firing back answers just as quickly as I threw the questions at him.

Brianna brings my inquisition to an abrupt halt.

"Timeout, timeout," she says with the hand movements. She turns to me. "Can I have a word with you in the ladies'?" she whispers with her brow furrowed.

"Yeah," I say knowing she is about to express her opinion about behaviour, which I could do without, but I get up and allow her to get up too.

"We'll just be five minutes," Brianna says sweetly to Michael, giving him an apologetic smile. He smiles in return but can't hide his confusion. Brianna then proceeds to poke me in the back to direct me to the ladies', as if I had no idea where the toilets were in our favourite restaurant. I jump at each jab, which in turn elicits funny looks from other diners. By the time we get to the ladies', I'm pretty annoyed. No one else is in here apart from us, not that I care. Brianna waits until the door is closed to round on me. "What the hell was that all about?" she demands.

"I was getting to know him," I say with a shrug.

"Getting to know him? That was borderline harassment!" she says incredulously.

"He looks just like someone I've seen before," I admit.

"He's not Nicholas or whoever the hell you said. He's Michael! The poor bloke couldn't even eat with all your questions!" she says with a hushed but irate tone.

"It looked like he ate okay to me," I say with a wavering voice. I watched him eat. He appeared to enjoy every mouthful. I know that food makes vampires sick, but I'm meant to know they don't exist.

"Are you kidding? I've eaten two courses while Michael has more than half of his starter left to eat! I don't know what has happened to you recently, but this isn't like you at all," she says waving her hand at me. "For the past month, you've been acting so odd. What is wrong with you?" she retorts with her fists pushing down at her sides and her neck extending out towards me. She's angry with me, and again, it's something that doesn't make any sense. She's never used this tone and behaviour with me before. It's reserved for jerks like ex-boyfriends and terrible drivers when she's a passenger in Anthea. I'm none of these things; I'm her best friend, and I don't deserve this kind of backlash. I really should just walk away without saying a word, but I feel I have to say something.

"Thank you so much for being my best friend and so understanding," I say pulling the door open and leave the ladies'.

"Rosannah," Brianna calls after me sympathetically, but this suddenly turns to panic as I march my way over to *Michael*. He looks utterly lost as I dig through my purse.

"That should cover what I've had," I say as I slam £30 down on the table.

"Rosannah, I'm sorry," Brianna says as she reaches us, but I ignore her and leave the restaurant. She doesn't follow me, for which I'm glad. In my angry marching state, it only takes me five minutes to get back home. I slip my shoes off and curl up on the couch with Marmalade and spend the rest of the

evening watching junk TV, wondering what
happened to my life.

CHAPTER THREE

Brianna

We walk into Michael's apartment silently after our evening out with Rosannah. I have no idea what has gotten into her lately. I have been worried about her, but Rosannah is the kind of person who will only tell you what's wrong if she wants to, and that's not very often at all. She's a very closed and private person when it comes to her feelings, and I know that no amount of asking her will get her to tell me what's wrong. I've learnt it's best to let her tell me in her own time, but tonight it was almost as if she wanted me to press her. I feel bad about having a go at her, but I'm so protective of Michael. I've never been as into a guy as I am with him. He was that shocked by her behaviour that he couldn't even finish his meal. I shake the thought away and focus on Michael. He doesn't turn any lights on and walks over to the couch by the far wall. He plonks himself down in the middle of it. The curtains are wide open, and the only light coming in is from a street lamp outside. Once I've taken my coat and shoes off and put my bag down, I sit down on the other couch.

We can have moments like this. Sitting on separate couches, seemingly ignoring each other while Michael's body is screaming to fuck me and mine screams back to be fucked. When it comes to sex, Michael is the perfect lover, and he gives as good as he gets. He's a split right down the middle kind of guy. Not a selfish jerk who breathes his bad breath all over you while he's pumping his tiny prick into you, thinking he's God's gift to women, oblivious to you lying there bored out of your mind. While you stare at the ceiling barely feeling anything but his weight crushing you. You know the type; the ones who promise you they'll eat you out after you gobble them off, but within seconds of them coming in your mouth, they fall fast asleep. That was all the experience I had ever had, and I thought that all guys were like that, but not Michael. He completely changed my mind and perspective. He makes sure I get my fair share of orgasms. Michael also has the right level of roughness and just seems to know my boundaries without me saying.

Michael flicks on the TV with the remote and puts it on the armrest to his right. He sits there with his legs open, his left hand resting next to him and his right hand sitting on his thigh. He's dressed in a casual pale blue shirt with black trousers. I love him in trousers. It shows just what he has when he's sat like that because his trousers always bunch up at the top as if they're cradling him. I can grope him easier too, feeling all of him through the material. But this guy is so highly sexed that groping is only for behind closed doors because it always leads to fucking.

The Amazonian rain forest is on the screen in front of me, but with Michael sat the way he is, I can't concentrate on it. This man turns my mind to mush. How I manage to keep any composure around him, I don't know.

Glancing every so often at the clock, I can see that Michael is engrossed in whatever he's watching. After twenty minutes, he gets up and stands in front of me.

The light from the TV behind him shows only his silhouette. My breathing becomes shallow with anticipation as I watch him slowly undo his shirt. As each button is undone, it reveals more of his rock-hard chest and stomach. Michael is an avid runner, and it shows. With painstaking slowness, he undoes his sleeves keeping his eyes fixed on mine.

A man stripping has always made me cringe. It's usually done in such a corny way and involves idiotically prancing about and hideous wiggling, but with Michael, it's all purely about me. Showing me just how much he wants me and slowly winding me up in the process. You can see the desire and longing on his face and in his eyes. His mind is all about our needs and nothing else.

He lets his shirt slide down his arms and fall to the floor. He undoes his belt and pulls it out of the loops in one swift motion. Holding it out to the side, he drops it onto the floor. Neither of us looks away to see where it lands. Undoing his trouser buttons, my breathing hitches and he lets out a light sigh.

"Oh, you're just dying to see my cock, aren't you?" he asks with a half-smile. He knows the answer but is teasing me. My voice has stopped working, but I eagerly carry on watching him. He drops his trousers, which pool around his ankles. I can't take my eyes off his. I'm hypnotised.

He steps out of his discarded trousers and walks over to me. Dropping to his knees in front of me, his hands slide under my dress and up my thighs. He grabs the elastic of my thong, and I lift my ass for him slip it off. I don't need directions or orders; I already know what is expected of me. It's a gut instinct, and even though Michael has a dominant side and being submissive isn't my thing, I have no objections if Michael orders me around in the bedroom. Surprisingly, I relish in it.

Grabbing my feet, he puts my legs over his shoulders. "This is where I like your thighs, on either side of my face," he says as he nips his way down the inside of my left thigh. I suck in a breath at each one, growing moist as he nears his destination.

When he reaches it, he rams his face between my legs, and I moan. His tongue starts lashing harshly at my opening. He pulls back slightly and looks up at me. "Your cunt tastes so sweet. Always so wet," he murmurs, his lips hovering just above my mound. I shudder at his words. He's not ashamed or embarrassed to talk dirty to me, and I love it. Keeping eye contact with him, I watch as he rams his face back to my throbbing pussy. I shamelessly wrap my legs around the back of his neck and ride him. His tongue beats my clit into submission, and within minutes, I come, crying out in pure ecstasy. Breathing heavily, I watch him stand up with my juices around his mouth. He licks his lips and takes his boxers off.

Looking down at his erection, he takes it in his right hand. Slowly, he starts to massage it, running his hand up and down his huge length. "Is this what you want to see?" he asks looking back up at me. "Me with my rock-hard cock in my hand?" he asks, his voice starting to strain.

"Oh, yes," I breathe.

"Take your dress off," he commands as he continues to massage himself. I can't help but obey. I get up and pull my dress up over my head, dropping it onto the floor. "Good. Now take off the bra," he murmurs. I unclip the back. "Slowly," he chastises. I take each strap off as slowly as I can manage and drop it to the floor. Michael sucks in a deep breath. "Now, lie down on the couch on your back and wait," he orders. I lie down, and he disappears for a couple of minutes. He reappears with a condom on his mighty cock. He climbs on top of me and my legs eagerly open to welcome him. As he lowers himself, I wrap my legs around him. "My, my, my, you're eager to be fucked, aren't you?" he teases.

"You have no idea," I murmur as I grab the back of his neck and pull his lips down to mine. His tongue licks at mine, and the end of his cock finds my slick entrance. Solid muscle and hard sex slam into me, hard. I moan with relief into his mouth as my hands find their way down to his flexing ass. He pulls back from our kiss to look at me.

"That's right. Moan for me," he says through gritted teeth. "Your tight little cunt loves me pounding it," he groans as he starts sliding in and out of me. Each stroke of his cock pushes me harder and faster towards my climax.

"Yes, oh God, *yes,*" I manage to get out as an orgasm builds. The end of his cock always rubs the right spot. My breathing becomes frantic as my muscles clench up and I come. "*Yes,*" I hiss as the orgasm rolls on. Michael doesn't stop and keeps going.

CHAPTER FOUR

Rosannah

It's a bright, sunny Monday morning when I walk into work. I didn't knock for Brianna because I've been dreading it, dreading facing her. We've never had an argument or even raised words. Saturday was a first and I hope an only occasion. When I see Brianna, she smiles apologetically at me, and my nervous energy melts into a laugh.

"We have a very busy day ahead. Here are your leads," Marie says, handing paperwork to me and interrupting us. We don't get a chance to say much to each other and work flat out until it's time to leave for lunch. As soon as we're outside, Brianna gives me a big hug.

"I'm so sorry. I've been feeling awful. Please forgive me," she says. I hug her back and sigh.

"Of course, you're forgiven," I say. She laughs and releases me. Linking arms, we walk to the cafe. "Is that why you look so tired?" I ask.

"Would it insult you if I said no?" she replies cautiously.

"No." I giggle as we walk into the cafe. We head to our usual table, but it's taken by a guy with his back to us. I can't see his face, but something about him feels familiar. Brianna tuts at the back of his head and pulls me over to a table near a window. Even though Brianna will bitch about anyone who sits in our usual spot, all she'll do is tut at them. And at the back of their head at that because she couldn't do it to their face.

"Usual, ladies?" asks Mike, who has just walked over to us.

"Yes, please," Brianna replies. We sit down and the sun shines through the window on us.

"So, why are you tired then?" I ask as Brianna yawns. My eyes dart over to the guy at our usual table. There's something about him that I can't put my finger on.

"Do you really have to ask?" Brianna laughs. It quickly dawns on me, but Brianna still indulges. "It's all this sex with Michael. He can go all night and doesn't even break a sweat." She sighs. I know exactly what that's like. I push the thought away with great difficulty and focus back on Brianna.

"Are you complaining?" I ask with a raised eyebrow.

"Definitely not!" She laughs.

Once our lunch arrives, we stop talking and stuff our faces. The guy who's sat at our usual table gets up and goes to the till to pay. I still can't see his face, but I watch him avidly as he reaches into his back pocket to get his money out. Once he's paid, he turns and heads toward the exit. *Oh, my God.* Piercing green eyes flash to mine as I jump up and run over to him.

"Alex!" I exclaim as I throw my arms around his neck.

"Er, yeah?" he says cautiously. I pull back from him expecting to see a smile, but he looks so confused.

"It's me. Rosannah," I exclaim. I'm so happy to see that he's alive.

"Do I know you?" he asks, looking me up and down. He doesn't know me. I'm mortified. Now, this has to prove that my time with Raphael definitely didn't happen, but then how do I know who this guy is if he didn't come to rescue me from Raphael's? Good God, I must be going insane.

"Sorry, I got you mixed up with someone else," I say and turn towards Brianna, who looks truly shocked. Her mouth is hanging open, and her eyes are wide. I dash back to my seat and sit down. "Stalker much?" Brianna leans over and mutters to me.

"I thought he was someone else," I reply with a shrug.

"Oh my God, he's coming over. What have you done?" she whispers at me in panic. When he reaches our table, I pretend I haven't seen him. *Real mature, I know*.

"Ahem," he says trying to get my attention. I slowly turn to look up at him. "I wasn't complaining," he says with a smile. "Are you free this evening? I make a mean spaghetti Bolognese," he says with a cheeky smile. Wait, what? Is he seriously asking me out on a date?

My brain goes into overload, and I can't think straight. "Oh, I can't," I blurt out. He looks disappointed, and Brianna kicks me under the table. "Ah," I say and rub my leg glaring at her.

"Of course she's free," Brianna says, grabbing a pen from her bag and a napkin from the table. "Here's her address," she says as she scrawls it down. "Pick her up at eight." She smiles as she hands it to him.

"I'll see you then." He smiles at me and leaves.

"Brianna, I can't believe you just did that!" I say incredulously.

"Oh come on, he was so into you. Besides, it's about time someone ruffled your sheets." She laughs.

"Keep your voice down," I chastise.

"Oh, come on. If this cafe isn't used to us by now, I'd be surprised." Brianna laughs. Don't you just love how she's included me in this? I give her an unimpressed look. "Oh, your expression is hilarious!" she says and laughs harder.

Once we're finished, I go and pay Mike. When I come back, Brianna is still laughing. I leave her there and walk back. She chases after me, and we enter work.

"Rosannah's got a hot date," she announces to Marie when she appears from her office. Marie raises her eyebrows but smiles.

"How lovely. Anyone I know?" she asks.

"Probably not but he's gorgeous." Brianna smiles.

"Big deal. I have a list of ladies as long as my arm waiting for a piece of this," Paul boasts as he gestures at his body. We all burst out laughing.

"They're waiting in that special place. You know the place, it's in your dreams." Brianna laughs.

"Whatever. It's true, you know," he sulks.

"Of course, it is," she says, trying to keep a straight face.

The time to leave comes around much too fast and the journey home is a nightmare. I'm bombarded with all sorts of dating etiquette from Brianna. Even outside her door, she's still going on.

"You can have a peck on the cheek and maybe on the lips. No, definitely on the lips but certainly no tongues. Or maybe just the cheek, you don't want him to think you're easy," she tells me. I'm glad when her mum saves me. She can see that I need saving.

Once I get in, I feed Marmalade and speak to my mum. I don't tell her about my date with Alex. She'd be all over it like a hot rash, and I won't hear the end of it.

I shower and then try to pick out an outfit. I want to be as covered up as I can but still look nice. I opt for a pair of dark blue skinny jeans, a black silk tunic, and a dark green crocheted cardigan. I throw it all on and team it with black pumps. Once I'm completely ready, I sit and wait on the couch with Marmalade. Time ticks by agonisingly slow. Why does time seem so slow when you're waiting for something? My mind begins its assault over the topic of my date. My nerves are through the roof. Bloody Brianna! I'm losing my bloody mind; the last thing I want or need is a date! The doorbell rings. Oh my God, he's here! I get up in a panic but try to breathe deeply. With jelly legs, I walk to the door and look through the spy hole. It's Alex. I don't know who else I was expecting to see. Marmalade runs over as I open the door.

"You look stunning," Alex says with a smile. "And who's this pretty little lady?" he asks as he crouches and strokes Marmalade under her chin.

"Her name is Marmalade." I laugh. "How did you know she was a she?" I ask as he stands up.

"Well, I had a fifty percent chance of getting it right." He laughs. "Marmalade?" he quizzes.

"It's a long story. Maybe I'll tell you about it someday." I giggle.

"I look forward to it," he says with a small smile. We stand in silence for a moment. "This way," he says and holds his arm out for me to take.

"Give me a couple of minutes," I say. After saying a quick goodbye to Marmalade and locking the door, I link arms with Alex and let him lead me down to his car. It's an emerald green Mazda Rx8. It complements his eyes in quite a striking way but how typical.

We're silent in the car as he drives to the other side of town. I have no idea what to say, so I stare out the window and watch the buildings and people go by. After a while, Alex slows down and pulls into the driveway of a grey detached house. Nothing much to say about it really; it's just a house. Nothing like Raphael's...oh.

"Are you okay?" Alex quizzes me.

"Yeah I'm fine," I say, putting on the realest smile I can conjure up. Alex grins and gets out of the car. He's the perfect gentleman, coming around to open my door then taking my hand and helping me out of my seat. He leads the way into his home. The door opens straight into the left side of the front room.

"Would you like anything to drink?" Alex asks, switching on the lights.

"A glass of water would be fine." I smile.

"No wine?" he asks, surprised.

"Maybe later." I laugh.

"Well, make yourself at home and I'll warm up dinner," he says as he gestures to a small black couch. He walks into the kitchen through a large connecting archway. I sit on the left side of the couch and look around the front room. It's no bigger than mine. The lighting is dim and the colours are dull. Pale khaki green covers the walls, and the carpet is a dark grey. A steep staircase dominates the left wall, and there's barely any furniture in here. This couch, a tall lamp, a coffee table, TV stand, and TV are all that's in here. It all looks pretty dated, too. Suddenly, a glass of water appears in front of my face. "Here you go," Alex says warmly. He sits next to me. "Dinner will be about ten minutes." He smiles. "So what do you do?" he asks

"Well, I'm a trainee estate agent," I say, half smiling.

"Is it good?" he asks.

"I have a wonderful boss, get paid well, and get to work with my best friend," I say, and my smile turns into a full one.

"Sounds pretty good. Where can I sign up?" he says with a laugh.

"It has its pitfalls, too. Paul, for one," I say shrugging my shoulders.

"Paul?" Alex queries.

"Yes, he's our newest trainee, and at seventeen, he's very forward in his...manner," I say, trying to hide my slight embarrassment.

"Oh, he's young and works in an office full of women. He probably feels intimidated," he says with a knowing grin. *Paul, intimidated?* I certainly don't think so. I just smile and nod my head. "Tell me about your family," he says, tilting his head to the side. I'm not comfortable with this subject, so to make it easier to discuss, I look down at my lap.

"I'm an only child as far as I know," I start.

"Really?" Alex asks. I can hear the surprise in his voice.

"Well, my dad ran off when my mum was pregnant with me. I've been told different versions of events over the years, but I'm certain my mum scared him off. She's quite the handful. All I know about my dad for sure is that he's dead," I say with a shrug.

"I'm sorry to hear that," Alex says sympathetically.

"Don't be. I should feel bad about it, and I do," I say admitting my guilt.

"You don't have to blame yourself for your father's death," he says compassionately.

"I don't blame myself for his death," I say feeling like I've said too much.

"What do you feel bad about then?" he asks with a knotted brow. I sigh in resignation.

"A couple of years ago, I did some research online and found that he had died five years prior. I couldn't tell my mum. She still has hopes that he'll come back one day, and I don't have the heart to tell her that he never will. That's what I feel bad about," I explain.

"Oh right, I see. You're looking out for your mother's best interest. I don't think you should feel bad about that," he says.

"My mum is all the family I have. She's an only child, too. My grandparents had died before I was born," I say.

"There could be more on your dad's side," Alex suggests.

"He was an only child as well, and his parents are dead, too. I found that out while researching. The only thing I can't be entirely certain about is whether he had any other children even though he never married. What about you?" I ask wanting to change the subject.

"I'm one of five brothers, and I have countless cousins," he says.

"One of five brothers? You all must have driven your mother nuts." I laugh.

"Completely." He grins. "My mum was desperate for a girl, so my parents kept trying. They gave up at number five," he says.

"What are all of their names?" I ask.

"Well, there's Andrew, David, Patrick, me, and then Christian. Andy has two girls, May and Sarah, and Patrick has a son called Connor. So I'm Uncle Alex, too." He grins. I can envision all of his brothers. I bet they're all gorgeous like he is, too. Not as gorgeous as Raphael, though. No one will ever be as gorgeous as he is because he's a figure of your *imagination*, I remind myself. Ultimate physical perfection can only be fictional. Alex falls short because he's real. "I'll just go and serve up," he says, pulling me from my thoughts. He leaves me sat there and returns a little while later. "I don't have a dinner table. Will trays do?" he asks bringing one with a plate on it over to me.

"I don't mind," I say, reaching for it. There's a trail of stream emanating from a neatly piled portion of bolognaise that sits on a bed of fusilli pasta. "I thought spaghetti Bolognese was meant to be served with spaghetti," I say as I take a forkful and blow on it to cool it down.

"It can be served with whatever you like really. It's up to whoever is making it, and I don't always follow the rules. Besides, pasta is easier to eat with bolognaise. If I were here on my own, then I'd make it with spaghetti and would be in quite a mess." He laughs sitting down next to me.

"So it's purely for practical reasons?" I ask as I take a bite.

"Yes." He laughs. It tastes absolutely wonderful.

"This tastes so good," I say surprised. "What's in here?"

"It's my mother's top-secret recipe. I'm not allowed to tell anyone. Don't ever tell her that I made it with pasta," he jokes. He thinks I'll meet his mum one day? *Whoa, awkward.*

"I won't." I try to laugh. We sit in silence for a moment when he suddenly sighs.

"Is it sad to admit that the hug I got from you is the only action I've had for a very long time?" he asks with a chuckle.

"You think that's sad? I've never even had a date before," I say laughing with him.

"Really?" he asks surprised.

"Apparently, this Virgo girl is way too fussy according to her mother," I admit, shaking my head.

"Virgo, hey? I'm a Capricorn. We're meant to gel very well." He smiles.

"You're into star signs?" I ask trying not to laugh. I look at my plate. I've managed to eat most of it already! I've been shovelling in mouthfuls while he's been talking.

"You could say that," he says with a wry smile. Another silence envelops us. I hate awkward silences.

"You have a lovely home," I say, trying to get the conversation moving again.

"By lovely, you mean sparse?" He laughs. "I don't spend much time here. Only to sleep and eat, really. I have a shop and spend a lot of my time there."

"What kind of shop do you have?" I ask eating my last mouthful. If he mentions anything to do with witchcraft, then I'll probably die.

"A magic shop," he says. I choke on my food. "Geez, are you okay?" he asks with concern. I grab my glass and down the remaining water.

"I'm fine," I croak. "I just swallowed down the wrong hole," I say and try to smile. A *magic* shop? How could I know anything about this guy? This makes the whole *Raphael* thing even more confusing!

"It's not a real magic shop. Just silly tricks and stuff," he says with a shrug of his shoulders. That's not why it freaked me out! "Let me take your plate. I hope you like vanilla cheesecake."He takes my tray and gives me a curious look. Doesn't he mean New York Style Cheesecake? Never mind.

"I love it." I smile as he heads into the kitchen. After a few minutes, he brings over a plate with a slice on it and a spoon. I tuck in as soon as it's in my hand. It's heavenly. "Is this another secret recipe?" I ask.

"Yes, it is." He smiles knowingly.

"You're a good cook," I compliment him.

"It's all down to my mother. All of my brothers can cook. We can sew, too." He laughs.

We idle chitchat through our dessert and for some time afterwards. Before I know it, the evening has gone, and it's time to go home. The drive back is a quiet but comfortable one. Alex walks me up to my front door. "I had a lovely evening. Thank you." I smile at him. I genuinely did.

"You're welcome. When can I see you again?" he asks with a wry smile.

"I'm not too sure, but I enjoyed hanging out," I reply.

"Oh, come on, you have nothing to lose. Shall we say Thursday?" he asks a little too eager. *Fantastic.* Now it's going to be too difficult to say no to him. I'm not overly attracted to him even if he is quite pleasant and handsome. Another date should be okay, I guess? I can tell him gently then that I want to be friends.

"Okay," I say trying to smile.

"Same time but at yours? I'll bring dinner and cook again." He smiles.

"Sounds perfect." I grin. He leans forward and kisses me on the cheek. I'm surprised by the sentiment but smile sweetly as he pulls back. He matches my smile and heads down the stairs. I head inside to a meowing Marmalade. "Where was my backbone when I needed it?" I ask her.

CHAPTER FIVE

Rosannah

The following day at work is exactly how you would expect it. A nightmare. Brianna was on me as soon as we were in Anthea. I don't know how I got away with it, but I refused to tell her anything until we were at lunch. So the morning at work comprised of Brianna sulking and Paul giving a running commentary on it. When Brianna wasn't sulking, she was throwing insults at Paul who batted them away as if they were tennis balls and he was a pro player. At one point, Marie came storming in.

"For goodness' sake, will you two stop it? This is an estate agents, not a playground. You're acting like children!" she had exclaimed in frustration. She had then stormed back into her office, slamming the door shut behind her. I sat there speechless while Paul sniggered to himself and Brianna scowled. We worked in silence from then until lunch time.

Brianna drags me to lunch without even telling Paul where we're going. Not really much point. We always go to the cafe for lunch, and Paul has a bad track record for passing on messages. Once we're settled at our usual table and have our lunch, Brianna strikes.

"Tell me everything," she demands.

Recalling the date has a sour déjà vu feeling to it.

"He definitely likes you," Brianna tells me.

"How do you know?" I tease.

"He asked you out and then asked you out again."
She laughs and slaps my knee. She had been like this
about Raphael. But had she really, though?

Once we've finished lunch, we head back to work.
After a hectic afternoon, it's now evening and I'm sat
at home, nestled on the couch with Marmalade.
Thoughts of Raphael enter my mind. Is it strange to
miss a fantasy? I have tried with all my might to
revisit Raphael in my sleep, but all I get is black.
Nothing but vast empty space. I'm desperate to see
Raphael again even if it's in the land of nod.

I switch the TV off and head to bed. Marmalade
curls up on the window ledge as I pull the covers up
around my neck.

When I wake up, it's the middle of the night. It's
pitch black and the first thing I notice is that the
bedding smells different. This isn't my bed. I freeze.
Where the hell am I? A sigh resonates to me.
"Raphael?" I ask in disbelief as I sit up, bringing my
knees to my chin and clutching the duvet. Light fills
the room with the click of a switch. I'm blinded
momentarily until my eyes focus. Taking in my
surroundings, I realise I'm back in my prison. At the
foot of the bed stands Raphael. He climbs on the
footboard and crawls slowly up to me. His eyes
fixated on mine. He stops with his hands on either
side of my thighs and his face millimetres from mine.
He tuts.

"Rosannah, where did you go?" he says slowly, his
lips so close I can almost taste them. "I've been
waiting for you. *So* patiently waiting for you." He sits
back on his heels; his hands slump into his lap and his
head hangs. "I'm..." His head snaps up, eyes as black

as the night. "Disappointed," he snaps as he lunges at me.

I wake up in a cold sweat with a start. Fumbling for the bedside light, I switch it on and sit up. Marmalade looks displeased on the window ledge. I look around the room and see I'm home. It was just a dream. That's all my Raphael is—a dream. I flop back and let out a frustrated sigh. My Raphael isn't real, so why does my heart ache so much?

Wednesday at work passes by uneventfully, mainly because my next date with Alex is tomorrow. Brianna is probably saving her onslaught for after the date. Once I'm home, I greet Marmalade. "Yes, yes, I'm happy to see you, too," I say as I bend down and scratch behind her ears. She follows me into the kitchen where I sort her food out. "Right. Now to deal with Mother," I say with dread. When I look at the answering machine, I see that there are three messages. My heart suddenly pounds in my chest. Only my mum, Brianna, and work have my phone number. I know one message will be my mum, but the others wouldn't be Brianna or work. So who are they from? I press play and the usual message from my mum plays.

"End of message one. Message two." The message is silent except for a few crackles, but I can't hear any breathing. My hearts picks up. Could it be Raphael? No, it couldn't be! I keep driving myself mad thinking about him! *"End of message two. Message three."* The third message plays, and I stare at the machine in amazement.

"Hi, Rosannah, it's Alex. Something has come up for tomorrow, but I'm free this evening. I'll be there about seven. See you later."

"End of message three. You have no more new messages." I look at the clock and it's half six. Geeez! How did he get my number? Brianna, of course! He must have been the second message. Why the hell did I agree to another date with him? He's lovely but just not my type. *And what is your type?* Dreamed up psycho vampires? You're destined to be a lonely old lady with cats because *that type* just doesn't exist. Never mind that I need to get ready if Alex is coming over! It will be awkward, but at least I can tell him that I'm not interested and stop leading him on. I have barely enough time to have a shower, pick something to wear, and throw it on. I hastily blow dry my hair. *Ring.* My time is up. I quickly run a brush through my hair, throw it up into a messy highponytail, and look at myself once more in my floor-length mirror. I've thrown on light blue skinny jeans, a peach coloured blouse with a white vest underneath, and peach flats. *Ring.* Argh, I'm coming! I race to the door and open it. Alex is standing there with a bottle of wine in one hand and two covered plates stacked on the other. Oh, I can't turn him away when he's brought this over.

"Let me take that." I smile, taking the plates and heading into the kitchen. Marmalade dances around my feet but then dashes off.

"You look great," he says closing the door and following me. I put the plates down but the sound coming from the TV makes my blood turn cold.

"Breaking news. Crayfield Maximum Security Prison has had another deadly brawl. It's the third this year," I hear coming from the front room.

"I'll be just a minute." I smile at Alex as I turn to face him.

"I'll get all of this started." He smiles. I race into the front room and stare at the TV.

"There's been no confirmation on the number of dead, but sources close to the prison report there could be as many as fifteen." I feel physically sick, but I know it's not Raphael. I close my eyes tight. Vampires don't exist. Vampires don't exist. Vampires don't exist. Vampires don't exist. Vampires don't...

"Here you go." Alex is by my side handing me a glass of wine and pulling me out of my chanting thoughts. I gulp down most of the glass in one go. "Whoa, steady there. Take it easy," he warns.

"It's been a very stressful day," I say forcing a smile and ignoring the burn in my stomach.

"Dinner's in the oven." He smiles.

"You worked it out all right?" I ask.

"Well, it wasn't that hard. Although I did call you to ask where some things were, but when you didn't reply, I looked around and found them myself." He shrugs. I blush with embarrassment and go and sit on the couch.

"Oh, I'll turn this crap off," I say grabbing the remote and holding it up to the TV.

"May I?" Alex asks holding his hand out. I hold it out to him, and as he grabs it, his fingers brush my hand. Something flashes in his eyes, but he turns to the TV before I can try to figure out what it was. He punches in a number and up comes the eighties channel. A Hall and Oates song plays, and we chitchat while the dinner is warming up. I take occasional tiny sips of my wine while nodding to the music and what Alex is saying. *When are you going to tell him?* Alex looks at his watch. "I'm just going to plate up." He smiles, getting up and then disappearing into the kitchen. I let out a big breath, and Marmalade appears from behind the couch.

"So, that's where you've been hiding?" I laugh as she jumps up onto the window sill.

"Here we go." Alex puts a plate on the glass coffee table in front of me. This time, he's cooked lasagne.

"Thank you." I smile.

Picking up the fork that's on the plate, I dig in. It tastes fantastic and turns out to be another secret recipe. In no time at all, I've finished my plate and tuck into dessert when it's brought out, which is a modest fruit salad. Once finished, and with Alex's insistence, I do nothing while he washes everything up. He puts it all away leaving my kitchen literally how he found it. Alex then plonks himself down next to me on the couch, and he gets so close that my nerves kick in. I take a swig of my wine to wash them away. Placing my glass back onto the table, my eyes travel down to his thigh, which is touching mine.

"I really like you, Rosannah," Alex admits as he takes my hands in his and runs his thumbs over my palms. "Look at me," he says softly. *Don't look at him; don't look at him.* I look up. Damn it. He holds me with a deep green gaze. A hand leaves mine and cradles the back of my head. Oh, crap! He leans forward to kiss me, but I jump up. What the hell is wrong with you? Alex is no Raphael, but at least he's real! "We can go slowly if you want," Alex says, oblivious to my inner turmoil.

"I can't do this," I blurt out.

"I'm moving too fast. I'm sorry," he says standing up and taking a step towards me.

"No, that's not it. You're a really nice guy, but I just don't want this. I've wanted to tell you all evening," I say feeling awful. I can see the rejection flash across his expression. He puts on a poker face and gathers his plates. Saying nothing, he leaves, closing the door quietly behind him. Damn it. I run after him, opening the door and call after him, but he doesn't respond.

The following day when I meet Brianna, she gets all excited about the date that I'm meant to be having this evening. I wait for lunch to tell her the news. "He came over last night," I say quietly.

"What? And you didn't tell me?" she shouts.

"Keep your voice down. We get enough odd looks as it is, no thanks to you," I chastise.

"Well, what happened?" she asks eagerly.

"Something had come up for tonight, so he came over last night. He brought over dinner and wine. He cooked the most wonderful lasagne and left the kitchen spotless," I say with a sigh.

"What a perfect gentleman. Just like Michael," she swoons.

"It all went wrong, though," I say dropping my head.

"Why?" she asks, her brow knitting.

"He tried to kiss me, and I kind of freaked out." I sigh.

"A really hot guy comes to your place, cooks, cleans, and tries to kiss you, and you freak out? Are you out of your mind?" she asks incredulously.

"I didn't even want to date him," I say crossing my arms and scowling at her.

"I know you didn't have much choice about date number one, but you did with date number two. Why did you agree if you didn't want to date him?" she asks.

"He made it kind of hard to say no. I tried to pluck up the courage all evening to tell him, but when he tried to kiss me, I had no choice," I say feeling awful again.

"How did he take it?" she asks carefully.

"He left without muttering a word," I say cringing.

"Oh." Brianna winces.

We finish lunch in silence and get back to work, busying ourselves with our computers. At the end of the day, Paul asks the first non-innuendo question he's ever asked us.

"Are you two okay?" he asks, concern flashing across his face. Wow. I tilt my head to the side to consider his sudden show of emotion, and his brow falters. "Whatever it is, I like it. You two silent is heaven to my ears," he scowls and walks out of the office. That was short-lived. Brianna and I look at each other puzzled, and she shrugs her shoulders.

"See you tomorrow." I wave at Marie, who's in her office. She waves back, and we head home.

CHAPTER SIX

Brianna

My phone goes, and I pick it up after one ring.

"I'm here," Michael breathes down the line. It sends a chill down my spine.

"I'm coming down," I almost moan back. The line cuts dead, and I put my phone in my bag. "I'm off, Mum," I say as I head into the front room.

"When am I going to meet this boyfriend of yours?" she asks with her arms folded.

"Ugh," Cody complains. I stick my tongue out at him, and he pouts.

"Soon," I promise, kissing Mum on the cheek. I race out the door and down the stairs to see Michael's BMW waiting for me. I open the door and slip into the passenger seat.

"Hi," I breathe. Without saying a word, he places a firm hand on my right thigh and speeds away.

Fifteen minutes later, we're at his place.

"Anything interesting happen today?" he asks casually as I take my coat off. We have moments like this, too. A *how was your day, dear* routine.

"Well, Rosannah's date got moved to yesterday, so she told me all about it," I say as I sit down on the couch.

"Who did she go on a date with?" he asks handing me a drink.

"Did I not tell you?" I ask, puzzled as I take a sip of my drink. Rose, my favourite. I grunt in appreciation.

"No," he says.

"A hot guy named Alex," I say. Michael sits next to me, and I feel the cushion I'm sat on dips towards him. After a while, I look at Michael, who looks like he ready to kill someone. Whoa.

"He was nowhere near as hot at you," I gush. The anger drops from his face, but he's still not happy.

"Get this.He turns up at hers, he wines and dines her, cleans up after himself, and she rejects him," I say, raising my eyebrows and hoping to calm him a little. It works.

"What did he do wrong?" he asks perplexed.

"He tried to kiss her," I say taking another sip of my wine.

"That's a crime?" he asks.

"To her it is. She freaked out and he left without saying a word," I say.

"I can't blame him, "he says.

"I know, but to be fair, I did push her to go on the first date." I giggle. Michael laughs his deep chesty laugh and catches me with his eyes. He's got that look on his face. The *I'm gonna fuck you senseless* look. I look away and sip my wine. Don't get me wrong, I love that look and I love sex with this man, but I want more than that. Yeah, he kind of has the title of *boyfriend*—well, that's what I let my mum and Rosannah think—but it hasn't actually been made official or even discussed. I remember when we first met. I was picking some essentials up at Tesco. Staring at my shopping list, I was walking around without looking where I was going. It was only inevitable that I would collide with something, and sure enough, I bumped into something solid. I honestly thought I had walked into a pillar, but in a haze of embarrassment and with my eyes glued to the floor, I saw shoes and large ones at that. I was so mortified that I couldn't bring myself to look up at whom I had walked into, but I apologised profusely. "I'm so sorry. I wasn't looking where I was going," I said, my voice high-pitched and small. I cringed, turned on the spot, and power-walked away. I couldn't face hearing a response from whoever it was.

Once I was at the end of the aisle, I risked a look back to see a man who I could only describe as sex on legs staring at me where I had left him. I could have died when he started to walk towards me. His walk was fast and confident, his face full of determination. I panicked and walked off in the only direction I could go. After weaving in and out of several aisles, I stopped, took in some deep breaths, and turned back to see if I had lost him. A broad chest covered my line of vision, and I stumbled. A pair of strong hands reached out and had grabbed my shoulders to stop me falling. "I said I was sorry," I screeched, looking up at his face. It was Michael obviously.

"If you had waited, you would have heard me accept your apology," he said calmly.

"So why have you followed me?" I asked him, confused.

"I wanted to ask you out on a date," he said simply. It was at that moment that I knew I was totally in love with him.

"What are you thinking about?" Michael asks, snapping me out of my daydream.

"When we first met." I smile. I then frown knowing that I'm just a bit of fun to him.

"Was it that bad?" He laughs.

"No, I was thinking about something else then." I half smile. We sit in silence for a while. "Michael?" I ask breaking the silence.

"Yes," he answers slowly.

"My mum and Rosannah think you're my boyfriend," I say looking at him to gauge his response.

"The things we do aren't enough for you?" he asks seductively. No, they're not, but I don't want to scare him off.

"I enjoy what we do..." I say, leaving the sentence hanging.

"But?" Michael prompts.

"I wouldn't mind more," I say sheepishly. He takes my drink and walks off to the kitchen. Have I upset him? When he returns, he has a naughty look on his face. Maybe not...

"What do you mean by *more*?" he asks standing in front of me, locking me with his gaze. With Michael, there are times when I feel so openas if I could tell him anything.

"A relationship," I breathe.

"We already have one, "he says seriously. I giggle, but he still looks serious.

"I know that, but that's not the type I meant," I say with a half-smile.

"Do you want me to be your boyfriend?" he asks playfully.

"Yes," I blurt out.

"Okay then, it's official. I'm your boyfriend." He shrugs sitting back next to me. "You know, I really like having you around. Let's really push the boat out and have you move in with me," he says staring off into space. Fuck, did he just really say that?

"Well, err…" I'm lost for words. He reaches over and pulls me onto his lap to straddle him causing me to squeak. He pulls my face down to his and kisses me hard. I pull back to look at him. "My mum hasn't even met you yet," I protest.

"We'll sort that out." He grins.

"Okay, I'll move in." I smile. Wait until I tell Rosannah; she's going to freak!

CHAPTER SEVEN

Rosannah

This morning was a bit of a blur. Work has been on overload, and when lunch comes around, I'm pretty relieved. Partly because I need a break, but also because I'm desperate to grill Brianna. She's been acting weird today. On the way to work, she was *quiet*. Brianna is never quiet. She even talks in her sleep. How do I know this? We used to have sleepovers all the time. Not at Mum's, of course. She never allowed any of my friends over. It was so embarrassing. How could I explain to my friends that my mother thought they were ruining my chances of getting a boyfriend? We were eight! The sleepovers were always at my friends' houses, but their mums never complained. My mother said it was because I was the daughter of a rich woman. As a child, I found that hard to understand. Money meant absolutely nothing to me. I had no concept of what anything bigger than a fifty was. They were just numbers; words I couldn't see in any physical form apart from a piece of paper. The word *rich* was a conundrum to me, and I didn't get why my mother was so funny with my friends' parents.

"Earth calling Rosannah." Brianna laughs, bringing me back to the present. I look down to see my lunch has arrived. "Mike even waved a hand in front of your face, and you didn't respond. What were you thinking about?" she says as she takes a bite of her BLT.

"Never mind that. I know something is going on, so spill," I say picking up my fork and stabbing at my omelette.

"Michael asked me to move in with him," she says nervously. I stare at her for a moment. Is she joking? She doesn't look like she is, but I wouldn't put it past her. Brianna isn't a huge prankster, but she knows how gullible I can be and abuses that knowledge every so often. To be honest,though, I wouldn't appreciate this kind of joke. I'm sure that Michael is a lovely guy, but he looks so much like Nicholas that it freaks me out. I know Nicholas isn't real, which comes as a relief, but it's still weird, and Brianna has an idea as to how he makes me feel. How big an idea it is, I don't know, and I don't want to find out.

"What did you tell him?" I ask, trying to sound indifferent.

"I said yes." She smiles. She's not joking then. It's nice she's not joking but moving in with him? She looks so happy, and I don't want to ruin this for her. "I'm telling Mum tonight," she says with a weak smile. I stick on a huge smile, and it seems to cheer her up. She carries on eating happily, but I can't help but be a little worried. She's known this guy for five minutes, but then again, I've never seen her so in love. I hope to God that he doesn't hurt her.

The afternoon is just as busy as the morning. Time races by and before I know it, it's the end of the working day. Brianna and I travel home in silence. Once I've pulled up, we get out and head into the apartment block. "Why are you so quiet?" I ask her as we start to climb the stairs.

"I still have to tell Mum I'm moving out," she says, her face scrunching up in dread.

"Don't worry. It'll be fine. You're a big girl," I say. A smile flutters across Brianna's face.

"I know Mum is going to complain about not meeting him first. How is she going to be happy about me moving out if she hasn't even met the guy I'm moving out with?" she asks. He hasn't met Janice? That makes no sense.

"Why on earth hasn't your mum met Michael yet?" I ask incredulously.

"It just hasn't come up in conversation. Besides, we weren't an official couple until last night," she admits.

"What the hell? Are you crazy?" I ask. Brianna's eyes begin to fill with tears and her bottom lip trembles. Brianna really needs some sense knocked into her, but at the same time, I'm her best friend, and she's about to do something incredibly difficult. She could do with my support. I take a few deep breaths. "Do you want me there when you tell her?" I ask with a friendly smile. Brianna looks a little relieved, probably because of my change of tune.

"Thank you, Rosannah, but I need to do this myself." She half smiles.

"Okay, I'll see you on Monday unless you need me," I say heading up my stairs as Brianna opens her door.

Once I'm in my apartment, I sort out Marmalade and phone my mum. My mum is still badgering me about boyfriends. *Do make-believe one's count?* I wish. It's crazy; nothing that I thought happened with Raphael exists and that in and of itself leaves me feeling almost bereft. I head into the kitchen, open the fridge, and see a lonely slice of lasagne sat on a plate wrapped up tight with cling film. A pang of guilt hits me, but I still take it out, heat it up, and eat it. Afterwards, I have a lovely hot shower and throw on a vest and shorts ready for bed later. *Ring*. Marmalade and I jump in unison at the unexpected call at the door. Oh no, Brianna's evening must have gone terribly wrong. Without a second thought, I race to the door and open it, expecting to see her. Instead, Alex greets me. "Oh." The word escapes my mouth before I can stop it.

"Try not to sound too excited to see me." He laughs, but it fades as his eyes rake down my body. As his eyes meet mine again, I can see a hunger in them, and I half smile feeling incredibly awkward. "I know I've turned up uninvited, but I didn't like how things ended the last time I was here," he says with an apologetic smile.

"I thought you were busy tonight and that was why you came over yesterday?" I ask in suspicion.

"I felt so bad that I cancelled what had come up so I could come over and apologise," he says with a cheeky grin. Something else that doesn't make sense. If something comes up, then it usually means it's very important or made up. Let's say, for Alex's sake; it's the first. If he cancelled today because something important came up, then he wouldn't cancel that to come here now to apologise to me. That kind of suggests he lied yesterday and possibly planned to come here today as well. I'm not too happy about where my thoughts are going, but I'm not going to express them.

"It's fine, Alex. I feel really awful too,but I would like to be just friends," I say. Especially now when my trust for you has dropped considerably. His face drops a little.

"I don't want to be friends. I really like you, Rosannah," he says taking a step towards me. This isn't the way he should be reacting. Any self-respecting man would accept what I was saying!

"You're a great guy, but I just don't see you like that. If you're not willing to be friends, then we have to call it quits now," I say regretfully.

"I can't be just your friend, so I have to call it quits then," he says frowning and walks off. What the hell is up with him? My shoulders sag, and I close the door. I put the chain on and walk back into the front room. So I'm back where I started, feeling guilty again. *Ring*. Oh my God, he's back. I hope that he's realised that he's being a bit of a jerk. I walk to the door and look through the spy hole, but there's no one there. Okay, that's a little weird. I turn and take a few steps before it rings again. *Ring*. Oh, this is getting ridiculous! I storm to the door, take off the chain, and yank open the door. I'mintent on expressing annoyance at Alex when I'm stopped in my tracks. There, leaning against the door frame, is Raphael. In all his gorgeous glory. Dressed in his trademark black leather jacket, he stands there smouldering. It's then that I realise I'm not breathing. In a rush, I let out the air in my lungs and it dawns on me that I'm actually extremely pissed off to see him. Without saying a word, I put all my strength into slamming the door on him, but he's too quick. Of course. His foot blocks my effort in banishing him from my home. Damn him! With a quick push, he forces the door open causing me to stumble backwards. In a split second, he's shut and locked the door and grabs my waist as I take my last step. His touch almost stings, and I can't hold back the anger that rushes through me. Never mind seeing red, I see white. The fact that Raphael is a vampire does nothing to stop me from letting him have it. Jabbing him in the chest, daring him to stop me, I watch as he retreats slowly.

"Five weeks!" I growl in a voice I've never heard before. "For five long weeks, I lost my *goddamned mind*!" I screech. I drop my hand and watch as disbelief spreads across his face. My anger boils as I continue my rant. "There wasn't a single trace of you for five fucking weeks!" I scream at him.

"You could have stopped by," he says with a half-smile. The cheek of it! I swing for his face with all I've got. My palm hits his face so hard that the sound the collision makes is horrific. The adrenaline racing through my body cancels out any pain. "I deserved that," he says in a daze, skimming his fingers over where I've hit. His skin is still immaculate and shows no sign of trauma. It's as if nothing happened at all, and this winds me up even more. When he drops his hand, I swing again. The daze he's in dissolves, and he catches my arm with a lightning quick reflex and a tight grip. I try to yank my hand back, but it's no use.

"Get the hell off me!" I demand. He pulls me in and kisses me so aggressively it's painful. I try to wriggle free, but I don't have anything left to fight with. My anger has boiled over and dried up. I can't stop the tears that overflow and spill down my cheeks. He gets the idea and pulls back. With a firm grip on my shoulders, he tries to shake a bit of sense into me, I can see clearly now. "You can't just barge your way back into my life like this," I say sucking in air between sobs.

"Coming back was inevitable. I have been lost and desolate without you. I'm sor..." he begins, cutting off. His eyes widen a little in shock, and he stands there staring at me in silence. I can't imagine *sorry* being a word that Raphael has used much in his *existence*. Nor do I think he's said it in a long time. Raphael is never sorry.

"All you do is hurt me. This is a fine example. You play your tricks and your games. Turning up here after completely removing yourself from my life with one thing on your mind," I say. My voice turns small, my eyes on the floor, as I feel the full force of my embarrassment weighing me down.

"Look at me, Rosannah," he coos. With effort, I pull my eyes up to his. His eyes have taken on the faintest shade of a darker grey.

"I've never used you for sex, if that's what you mean," he whispers. He has that mysterious look on his face again. I'm still not sure what it is, but butterflies crowd my stomach and fire suddenly races through my veins. The need to have his lips on mine is almost painful. I reach up and pull his face to mine. His cool lips are hungry, and his tongue dips into my mouth. His hands wind up my top; he clenches at my back and groans. I start to ache and throb, growing moist. I need him there. As if answering my prayers, he rams a hand down the front of my shorts and buries two fingers deep inside of me. I gasp, and he growls. Pulling back from me, his eyes are jet black.

"You're so wet for me," he hisses. His thumb finds my tender clit and strokes in a circular motion while his fingers massage that sensitive place deep inside me. I start to moan as he picks up his pace. My knees go weak, and he cradles me with his other arm.

"Ah," I cry out clinging to his shoulders. My orgasm is imminent.

"That's it, moan for me. By the time I'm finished with you, I want you screaming out my name," he says through gritted teeth, and it's too much to bear. I come on his fingers, clenching him tightly with my muscles. Frantically grabbing at his shoulders, I cry out as each wave hits me. After they stop, Raphael places me back down on shaky legs and pulls his fingers out of me. He sticks them in his mouth, and his eyes roll back with a growl. Putting a hand on either side of my face, he pulls me to him. Resting his forehead on mine, he squeezes his eyes shut tight.

"I have got to get inside of you," he whispers almost in agony. I break away from him with a few steps backwards, and he watches as I lift my vest off over my head. Our eyes fix on each other. I then take my shorts and panties off, baring myself to him.

"Take me," I order. The words seemingly come from someone else because I feel almost possessed; possessed with desire. I watch as Raphael becomes a blur and emerges naked. With a couple of steps, he's with me. Wrapping his arms around me, he lowers me slowly onto the thick rug in the middle of my front room. Lying next to me, he nibbles my ear.

"I love how I make you fall apart, "he whispers. He bites my neck, and I cry out. As he sucks at the blood, he plunges his fingers back into me. I quicken instantly and come again. He licks my wound clean and pulls out. "So quick," he growls as he climbs on top of me. My knees part to let him in. Resting his hips between my thighs, he kisses me deep. Stroking his tongue with mine, he groans and pulls back from our kiss as he enters me hard. I look deep into his eyes as I yelp. He thrusts hard over and over. For hours and hours. I lose count of how many times I come and how many times I scream his name.

CHAPTER EIGHT

Raphael

The past five weeks have been one frustration after another. The day Rosannah left, I crawled into a dark shell and hoped to rot away. It didn't last long. The next day while in my study, a knock at my door pulled my attention to it. It was usually just a knock with no words. It had happened countless times over the previous few hours, and I usually ignored it, but I have my limits. "I said go away!" I yelled as my frustration got the better of me. I chastised myself for even acknowledging the world outside of my self-assigned prison.

"Raph, The Synod wants to see you," said a very anxious Evangeline from the other side of the door. In a split second, I was out of my chair; the door was smashed against the wall and I was facing her, snarling.

"You rang them again?" I growled in her face.

"No, they keep trying to call you," she said, panicked. I really did not want to deal with The Synod, but if I did not sort it out then and there, it would only get worse. I knew that at least one of them would be getting incredibly impatient.

"Well, this is just great," I yelled as I raced past her. I knew she probably had a hand in it. Anything happened and miss goody two-shoes could not help but try to be some kind of self-acclaimedGood Samaritan. She wanted to gain brownie points in hopes of becoming a member one day. She could dream on; none of us planned to leave the organisation anytime soon although I would not mind if Reggie left.

I ran out the front door and sprinted towards the main road, clearing the gate with one swift jump. I hit the ground running and didn't stop until I had reached Mathias' house. He opened the door as I stopped in front of it.

"I've been expecting you. Come in, dear boy," he said moving out of the way to let me in. I marched past him and made my way into his dining room, having taken notice on the way throughthat his wife, Maria, was happily watching TV in their living room. Once Mathias joined me, I turned on him.

"Why have you summoned me?" I asked with displeasure.

"Raph, we know that Rosannah *escaped*," he said. He was choosing his words wisely. "The Synod wants to move towards carrying out what it sees as necessary," he said carefully.

"What the hell do you mean by *carrying out what it sees as necessary*?" I asked him incredulously. "Besides, Rosannah did not escape. I threw her out."

"There are those of us who were worried about the situation, and now that Rosannah is free, we feel that something should be done in order to keep our integrity," Mathias said. That did not answer the question.

"There is no way on this earth that I will let anyone, vampire or otherwise, carry out anything to do with Rosannah. Especially Reggie!" I yelled. Mathias looked regretful but still continued.

"Reggie is not The Synod," he pointed out.

"You could have fooled me," I said with exaggerated sarcasm.

"My hands are tied. Unless you can come up with a better solution?" he asked.

"I'll erase any knowledge of me from her life and make it look like she was never away. The only human who will know about us is Rosannah," I said with regret. It meant that I would no longer exist in her world. The pain in my redundant heart ignited again at the thought.

"She could still tell people," he pointed out, still concerned about saving his own hide.

"I know that she won't tell anyone. Besides, who the hell would believe her?" I asked, hoping that would settle it. I only used the trump card when necessary.

"Okay, Raphael, I'll sort The Synod out and you sort Rosannah out. I'm putting a lot on the line by allowing this," he said with a grim smile. Without saying a word, I raced back home. Evangeline had the decency not to be there when I returned.

The following day, I had my work cut out for me. I visited Brianna and her family to brainwash her into thinking that Rosannah had never been away and that a valuation had never happened. I then headed for Rosannah's work and found the boy and Marie there early. I brainwashed them with the same story and changed my file, forging Rosannah's handwriting and shredding any other evidence. I then asked Marie if there was anyone who would have noticed Rosannah had been missing. She happily told me about a nearby cafe and Rosannah'smother. Made a quick trip to the cafe, missing Rosannah on her way into work. I brainwashed the owner and asked him about the other customers. I returned later to brainwash those, but in the meantime, I raced to Rosannah's to delete all the voicemails on her home phone. I found her mother's number and brainwashed her, too. All of the plans had been set in motion, and from then on, it should have been like I never existed. Out of all the things I have ever done, that was the hardest. I headed home and slunk back into my pit of despair.

A week after that, Lawrence returned from following Nicholas. I climbed out of my pit to greet him. "Hello, Lawrence," I said.

"So what happened with Nicholas?" a tactless Evangeline asked him. Lawrence winced, and I glared at Evangeline, who was completely oblivious to the pain Lawrence felt.

"I chased him until he stopped running. As we happened to be in South America, I knew of a place he could go. There's a therapeutic group of vampires there who specialise in vampire distress and mental health, in Chile. I was assured that he was in good hands, so I left him there," he said trying to put on a brave face, but I could see the pain in his eyes. Our brother Nicholas was broken, and it was agonising not being able to fix him. Lawrence knew it, and I knew it. It was also obvious that Lawrence was broken, too. He had returned with half of himself missing, probably feeling as if he had abandoned Nicholas. None of this fazed Evangeline. She had missed our brothers while Lawrence was gone, but once he had returned, she soon was complaining about him, which in turn caused her not to miss Nicholas.

For most of the following weeks, I was quiet and resided in my study. I ignored calls from The Synod and missed meetings. Lawrence knew something was amiss with me but had the sense not to question it. He knew deep down how desolate I was inside. Evangeline had filled him in about the sacrifice that I had made.

I am now sat in my study, alone with my forsaken heart. My thoughts are the same tireless ones that continue to play in its twisted tormenting loop.

Footsteps approaching the study door pull at my attention. "What do you want?" I ask not bothering to see if they are going to knock.

"There's been a development, Raph," Lawrence says quietly. A development? What could have possibly happened to move any of this on? I stride over to the door and open it. "Alex is back on the scene," he says looking at me, probably wanting to see my reaction. I do not give him one, even though the glimmer of hope that I may be able to get involved in Rosannah's life once again, even if indirectly, sparks in my chest.

"What has he been doing?" I ask flippantly.

"He's, ah, been taking Rosannah on dates," he says looking at the floor. Rage fills me, but I refuse to show any reaction.

"How many?" I demand deadpan.

"There have been two. She kicked him out after the last one, but it looks like he's heading over there tonight," he says as I walk towards the door. Kicked him out? That is the best thing I have heard in a long time.

"I thought you were meant to be keeping an eye on him? Why did you not tell me before?" I ask as I flash my jacket on.

"She was moving on. I didn't see it as a bad thing," he says cautiously.

"We both know that Alex is bad news. You also know how I feel about her. Put two and two together, for goodness' sake," I growl.

"Raph, don't do anything stupid," he warns.

"Since when does stupid apply to me?" I ask, dashing off before he can answer. I stop as soon as I am in the communal door of Rosannah's apartment building. Drawing air into my abandoned lungs, I am slightly unnerved at a scent I pick up. In amongst many, there is a light smell of musk mingled with a heavy undertone of sex. I dash up towards Rosannah's floor, relieved that the scent of sex ends a floor below. The musk, however, continues up and the source is revealed. I'm met by a very pissed off Alex.

"Oh, hey." He half smiles recognising me as he sidesteps me. I want nothing more than to rip his head off, but I have to see if Rosannah is okay. Alex is back on the scene for some reason, and Lawrence is incredibly unreliable to keep tabs on what this guy is doing all the time. This has now also presented me with a reason to step back into Rosannah's life once again. The Synod will be happy for me to keep an eye on her to aid in finding out what is going on with this walking death wish. Reggie will not be pleased, but I will pull out my trump card to get Mathias to put his leash back on him if I have to. Why did I not think of this before? Perhaps I thought Lawrence would be a better lookout. Although, the truth lies more in the fact that I was not able to function properly.

I wait for him to disappear and then ring Rosannah's bell. When I hear her heading to the door, I stand out of view. I have a feeling that she may not be so happy to see me and may not answer the door if she knows I am here. I mentally facepalm myself when she retreats, so I push the bell again. I smile to myself as she stomps her way over. I can picture her little frown marks and the brazen shade of red she gets when she is angry. I lean on the frame as I listen to her release the chain and unlock the door. She flings it open, and we both stand motionless, staring at each other in awe. Only the sound of Rosannah's heartbeat, racing as fast as a hummingbird's wings, hangs in the stifling air. She releases a held breath in a huge rush almost as if she has been punched in the stomach. Something then changes behind those big beautiful eyes of hers, and almost in slow motion, I watch as she lifts her hands to close the door on me. My foot is in the way before she has even started to push. I have needed this girl just as she needs air. Once dead always dead? A part of me died when she left the existence I call my life, and now it has blossomed back into life upon seeing her once again. I cannot let her shut me out, even though I threw her out of my world. I am as selfish as they come.

The door hits my foot and a mixture of horror and annoyance dots that pretty face of hers. With a controlled push of my arms, I force my way in. While she's stumbling backwards, I shut and lock the door. I am with her in a split second. I reach out and grab her waist to stabilise her, but she recoils like a venomous snake. She stalks forward, jabbing me in my chest.

"Five weeks!" she growls. "For five long weeks, I lost my *goddamned mind*! "she spits at me. I wince at every jab. Not because they physically hurt but emotionally, a powerful meaning sits behind each and every single one of them. She stops her finger assault and drops her hands to her sides. There is a fire dancing behind those big bright eyes that I have never seen before. The fierceness emanating from her is frightening. I stare at her wide-eyed, almost cowering from her. I am flabbergasted by how upset she is. I expected her to be angry but not like this. "There wasn't a single trace of you for five fucking weeks!" she screams at me.

"You could have stopped by," I offer with a smile of surrender. I see the slap coming a mile off but feel powerless to stop it. It happens with an incredible sound. It was hard, precise, and forceful. She meant every ounce of it, and it has me reeling. "I deserved that," I say reaching up to touch where she hit. When I lower my hand, she takes aim again. Why do I keep letting her take shots at me? I grab her wrist just as her palm is about to crash against my left cheek. She starts to struggle, pulling at her hand.

"Get the hell off me!" she yells. Passion ignites me, and I pull her into my arms, my lips meeting hers viciously. She still struggles, and I cannot bear it. I pull back and grab her shoulders. Tears cascade down her cheeks.

"You can't just barge your way back into my life like this," she sobs.

"Coming back was inevitable. I have been lost and desolate without you. I'm sor..." I leave the word hanging in the air through shock. It is a word I have not used for a very long time. What has this woman done to me? She has crept under my skin, crippled my resolve, and captured my heart. It is no one's fault but my own; I let her in. But I do not think I ever had a choice in the matter.

"All you do is hurt me. This is a fine example. You play your tricks and your games. Turning up here after completely removing yourself from my life with one thing on your mind," she whispers, her gaze centred on the floor.

"Look at me, Rosannah," I say with a soft shake of her shoulders. She slowly looks up at me through eyelashes soaked with tears. "I have never used you for sex, if that is what you mean," I whisper with a deep swelling in my chest. I feel ripped open and bare as I look at her, waiting for her to say something, but she reaches for my face and pulls me down to kiss her. The stress in her shoulders dissipates, and she melts into my arms. Her kiss soothes my weeping wounds. My hands dart underneath her top, gripping her back, desperate to feel her skin. I groan on contact. My erection comes almost instantly, and I have to be inside of her as if my very existence relies upon it.

CHAPTER NINE

Rosannah

I wake in the morning and roll over to reach for Raphael only to find he's not there. Have I been dreaming again? I sit up and rub the sleep from my eyes. I find myself naked and on my front room rug. All the events of last night flood my mind. It's overwhelming, but I make up my mind that everything did happen. I get up and check the flat to see if Raphael is still here. He's nowhere to be seen. Damn him! I pick up my strewn clothes and throw them into the dirty basket. I jump into the shower and start scrubbing. I don't know whether I'm angry or not. He's disappeared again, but I'm elated that he's back in my life.

Once I'm dressed, I have breakfast, but the doorbell interrupts me. I look through the spy hole and see it's Brianna. I open the door with a smile. I'm glad to see she's not upset, but she looks shattered. She pushes past me and heads into the kitchen. Flipping the kettle on, she proceeds to make herself a strong coffee—in silence. Once she's sat down on the couch in the living room and taken a few careful sips, she finally engages with me.

"Spill it," she demands.

"Spill what?" I ask, confused.

"Last night and all that sex you had," she says. *Oh, my God!*

"You heard that?" I ask sheepishly.

"I'd have to have been deaf not to hear *that*. I think the whole block heard you. The stories me and my mum had to make up to tell Cody what was happening up here was unreal. It's safe to say we all got zero sleep last night. Now I know how Michael's neighbours must feel," she moans, taking another sip of her coffee.

"I'm so, so sorry," I gush with embarrassment.

"Never mind sorry, just tell me all about it," she says slipping her feet out of her slippers and tucking them underneath her bum. It's then that I realise she's still in her pyjamas. I feel so awful but what the hell am I going to tell her? I had a gorgeous vampire screwing my brains out all of last night? You know the one, the one you were brainwashed into forgetting!

"Well..." I try to start.

"I thought you didn't like Alex, but you sounded like you *really* liked what he was doing to you last night." She giggles. Alex? Ohhhhh, she thinks I slept with Alex.

"I didn't sleep with Alex," I blurt out. Her eyes nearly pop out of her head. I slap a hand over my mouth. Damn it.

"Who was it then?" she asks eagerly. How am I going to explain this one?

"I can't tell you," I say regretfully.

"He isn't married, is he? Please tell me he's not," she asks riveted.

"No." I shake my head vigorously. "You know I would never do anything like that!" I say, offended.

"I know you wouldn't, but you're not giving me much to go on," she says. She's not meant to be able to figure this out!

"Was it a woman?" she asks, becoming gripped by her ideas.

"What? No! You're just as bad as my mother," I chastise her.

"Does your mother know about this mystery man?" she asks taking a big sip of her coffee. I shoot her a look. "Of course not. I know your mum would have a seizure if you broke the news that you'd finally popped your cherry," she says, taking another sip.

"It wasn't my first time," I say without thinking. Brianna almost sprays me with coffee.

"*Jesus,* Rosannah. You've been holding out on me. If you can't tell me who, then tell me what," she says, putting her coffee down. A vampire? I know that's not what she means.

"I know that when people talk about losing their virginity, they say it was pretty lame, but mine wasn't. I've only ever known mind-blowing sex," I say with a huge grin.

"Does he make you come?" she asks. I never thought I'd ever be having this kind of conversation with Brianna. Well, I've had loads with her, but I've always been the listener; now it's her time to listen.

"I've lost count," I admit, feeling slightly embarrassed.

"Does he make you come through sex?" she asks, completely immersed in our conversation.

"Yes, multiple times. He does it with his fingers, his mouth. He goes all night," I say gushing.

"I know exactly what that's like. Michael's an all-nighter, too." She grins. Michael! Ah, I'm more suspicious of him now that Raphael is back in my life, although I can't help but wonder if he's going to disappear again. I push the thoughts aside.

"Does he *bite* you at all?" I ask cautiously.

"No." She laughs. "Does your mystery man bite you?" she asks.

"You could kind of say that," I answer honestly. Worried that I may have opened a can of worms, I quickly change the subject. "How did it go with telling your mum about moving in with Michael?" I ask.

"It went fantastic. I'm moving out tomorrow. As well as to grill you, I came up here to ask if you would help," she says, looking at the ground.

"Of course, I'll help." I grin.

"Right then," she says, jumping up and grabbing her empty mug. "I'll see you tomorrow at about ten am downstairs," she says as she wanders off to the kitchen and washes up her mug. "It's going to be a busy day tomorrow, so please try not to have a sex marathon tonight."

"I shall try my best," I say trying not to laugh.

"Good. I'm going back to bed to catch up on the sleep I've been deprived of." She giggles and leaves, closing the door behind her.

CHAPTER TEN

Raphael

I race home, leaving Rosannah sleeping on the rug. I hate to leave her, but I need to get back. I do not want Lawrence or Evangeline asking questions. I was very foolish last night. I had only intended to check on Rosannah, but one thing led to another, and I couldn't help myself. When I arrive, Lawrence is home. "You are still here?" I ask in an attempt to sound casual as I join him in the kitchen.

"Well, I waited for you to come back. Anything you want to talk about?" he asks.

"No," I say deadpan. Lawrence raises his eyebrows questioningly but says no more on the subject.

"So Alex is still in one piece?" he asks.

"Yes," I hiss, taking off my jacket and hanging it up. Although I am somewhat reluctant to remove Rosannah's scent from my skin, I dash upstairs for a shower and put on fresh, clean clothes. When I come back downstairs, Lawrence is still lingering in the kitchen, and I can see he wants to ask me another question. But I sit down and read the newspaper that is lying on the counter, leaving him to stew. After a while, I have had enough of him watching me. "What?" I ask lowering the paper. He whizzes over and sits opposite me.

"If you didn't kill him, then what did you do last night?" he asks inquisitively.

"That is none of your business," I say lifting the paper back up.

"You were out all night," he says suspiciously. I drop the paper on the breakfast bar.

"What do you want me to say?" I ask irritated.

"Well, the truth would be nice." He laughs.

"I spent the whole night with Rosannah, okay? Screwing her brains out, okay?" I say hearing someone coming through the front door.

"It's nice to see you back to your usual obnoxious self." Lawrence grins. Evangeline then walks into the kitchen.

"You. You are now tasked with the job of following this *Alex,*" I say, stopping her in her tracks.

"I thought Lawrence was doing that," she whines, flicking her hair over her shoulder.

"He messed up," I say while Lawrence smirks. I turn to him. "You are still doing it, but she is supervising you," I tell him, wiping the smirk off his face.

"Oh, I'll do it on my own. I can't work with him. He's annoying," she says crossing her arms. Lawrence pulls a face at her. I fling my arm in front of her as she goes to launch herself at him.

"Lawrence, tell her where he lives," I say holding her back.

"I already know where he lives," she sulks and races off out the house.

"She's so touchy." Lawrence scowls.

"You do not make the matter any easier," I chastise.

"Why can't you watch Alex?" Lawrence asks.

"I have a duty to Rosannah," I reply.

"If that's what you call it." He smirks.

Several hours later, a very upset Evangeline returns.

"I'm outta here," says Lawrence before he disappears. Damn him.

"What is the matter, Evangeline?" I ask, not really wanting to know.

"I lost track of him," she says with a huff.

"You *lost* track? How did you manage that?" I ask incredulously. Vampires are hunting, killing machines. We *never* lose track of anyone or anything; unless the vampire is a complete moron.

"I don't know what happened. One minute, he was at his house, and the next, he was gone," Evangeline says throwing her arms up in the air.

"Do you think he knew you were watching him?" I ask.

"There's no way he could have known," she says resting her hands on her hips.

"Then whoever he answers to must have known you were watching and counted on your lack of ability to concentrate," I say walking into the hallway and putting my coat on.

"Where are you going?" she asks.

"I will be back soon," I say and race off to Lawrence's house.

He opens the door as I arrive. "We have another problem," I say walking past him. "Evangeline lost track of him," I say. He looks shocked but gathers himself up almost instantly.

"How did she manage that?" he asks.

"We both know that Evangeline can lose interest easily. It appears that this was taken advantage of. I was not sure what I was hoping for when I got her to help," I say to Lawrence. He nods in agreement.

"What's the plan?" he asks.

"For now, we will head to Alex's place. You lead the way," I say. Lawrence races off, and I follow.

Minutes later, we are hiding in a shadow of bushes opposite Alex's house. We do not have to wait long until his phone rings.

"Hello, Alex here," he says a little too joyously. I growl slightly in disgust.

"Who answers the phone like that?" Lawrence whispers.

"What is your development?" a robotic voice asks Alex down the line. I can hear their conversation with ease.

"I don't have any developments," Alex replies automatically. This is a clear indication that he is brainwashed.

"You went to see her again, did you not?" the robotic voice asks.

"Yes, but she chucked me out," he says. *That a girl.* I smile to myself.

"You know what you're meant to do. You are to go to her again but not yet. Something has cropped up. I will be in touch soon with your next instruction," the robotic voice says, and the line goes dead.

"Why on earth am I holding the phone?" Alex asks himself, quite confused. "I'm sure I'll remember soon enough who I was going to call," he says and then replaces the receiver. I race back home without saying a word, and Lawrence follows me. We are met with a stroppy Evangeline.

"Where did you go and why have you brought Lawrence with you?" she sulks.

"I went to find out more about Alex like you were supposed to do," I say taking my jacket off and heading into my study. Lawrence and Evangeline follow.

"At least we have some information this time," I say to Lawrence, who nods his head.

"What information?" Evangeline asks in her usual ditsy way.

"The one calling Alex's shots is a vampire and a cautious one at that. It looks like they communicate through phone calls using a voice distorter so they cannot be recognised," I tell her. Confusion spreads across her face.

"How do you know they're a vampire?" she asks.

"They were brainwashing him over the phone," I say.

"What about the spell that was cast on Rosannah?" she asks.

"I do not think he actually cast a spell on her. You know as well as I do that magic does not really exist. I do know that humans are incredibly gullible, and they can be led to believe most things if the idea is planted deep enough into their brains," I say.

"But they wouldn't have been able to brainwash Rosannah to believe Alex." She pouts.

"She fell for it because Alex wholeheartedly believed it. He behaved as if it was completely true," I say. She fell for that, but the idea of a vampire was too farfetched for her. Maybe she was in denial. "I still do not understand what this vampire would want with Rosannah?" I ask myself, pacing the floor.

"Am I off duty now?" Evangeline asks with boredom. I do not bother to explain that she was essentially fired hours ago.

"Yes," Lawrence and I say in unison. Evangeline pulls a surprised face and then bolts. I turn to Lawrence.

"Do you think you can handle keeping an eye on him this time?" I ask raising an eyebrow.

"Yes. As soon as he's on the move, I'll let you know." He grins and bolts, too.

CHAPTER ELEVEN

Rosannah

Ten o'clock the next morning comes around very quickly, and I make my way down to Brianna's. Knocking on the door, I feel slightly panicked. I'm going to be spending the day helping Brianna move into Michael's place. That means I'll be spending most of that time with him, too. If he makes any fast movements or does anything suspicious, then I'm going to freak. I don't know why I can't just accept that he's not Nicholas, but it's so hard when he practically has his face. I make a mental note to ask Raphael about Nicholas when I see him next. That's if I get to see him again. I push the unwelcome thought from my mind as I knock on Brianna's front door. Little Cody opens the door with a huge grin on his face. "You're very happy this morning," I say to him.

"My sister is moving out, and I'm getting her room." He smiles.

"But I thought you already have a room," I say.

"Yeah, but Brianna's is bigger, and mine can now be a playroom," he says.

"Get out of the way, pipsqueak," Brianna says as she lightly barges past him.

"Oi," he complains.

"His room isn't going to be a playroom. It's going to be Mum's office," she tells me with a roll of her eyes.

"I was talking to Rosannah. Go away!" Cody yells at Brianna while trying to push her out of the way.

"If you don't stop, then I'll tell Rosannah about how much you fancy her," she says with a wicked grin. Cody's face turns pink as he stares open-mouthed at her. This soon turns to anger.

"Urgh, I don't fancy Rosannah," he says with disgust and runs off.

"Brianna, you're so cruel," I say trying not to laugh.

"Little shit had it coming. Can you believe he's been jumping and dancing around singing 'my sister's leaving, hallelujah' since I told Mum I was moving out? Mum said he's only been doing it while I've been home."

"Shall we get started?" I ask her.

"Yes, of course. I've already boxed everything up, so all that's needed is totransport them. Michael is due any minute, and we're going to use his car, too," she says. A smile suddenly plays on her face, and I'm aware that someone is behind me. Taking a large sidestep around me, I can see it's Michael.

"All right, Rosannah?" he asks politely as he takes Brianna in his arms. I weakly smile and nod.

Once we 'reorganised, we get all of Brianna's stuff moved. It takes Michael and me two trips each to get it all to his flat.

"Brianna, who knew anyone could have so much stuff?" I joke as I put down the last box in Michael's front room.

"It comes part and parcel with Brianna." He grins as he pulls her into a hug and plants a kiss on her lips. I stand there uncomfortably as he proceeds to stick his tongue down her throat.

"I'll just make some tea," I say turning from them. Brianna soon joins me in the kitchen. "That was pretty steamy," I whisper.

"Oh, that's nothing." She winks at me.

"How does Michael like his tea?" I ask, intrigue wrapping its way around my words.

"Oh, milk and one sugar," Brianna answers and smiles obliviously. I go to get some milk from the fridge. I'mhalf expecting it to be full of blood, but I'm surprised to see that it's full of food, and there's no sign of anything vampiric. Some of it appears to be half eaten, too.

After I make Michael his tea, I take it to him while Brianna starts emptying boxes and making use of her allocated draws and wardrobe space. I watch intently as Michael takes a few sips of his tea after blowing into the mug. I stand there waiting for him to throw up. I find myself almost wishing he would, but this soon turns to horror. Not with him but with myself. It's clear now that I'm terribly wrong about him and feel quite guilty about it.

"Erm, are you okay?" he asks nervously.

"Yeah, that's some mean stare you've got going on there." Brianna laughs lightly clapping my shoulder.

"Oh. I just wanted to make sure you liked your tea," I say trying to smile my mortification away.

"It's great. Just how I like it." He smiles.

I spend the rest of the afternoon helping Brianna unpack and put her stuff away. I have the occasional sneaky peek at Michael, who by this time has drunk three cups of tea and eaten two biscuits and a sandwich. No throwing up at all. He's definitely human and certainly isn't Nicholas. I must have been so desperate to see Raphael that I grasped at anything that would point to him being real. Poor Michael just became a target for unintentional false accusations. I didn't know just how desperate I was to see Raphael until last night. I was completely blinded by it.

Brianna, Michael, and I spend the evening laughing and joking sat on their front room floor. It feels and sounds weird to say 'their,' but that's how it is now. Soon our messing around turns to them starting to look really cosy, and I feel like a third wheel.

"I'm going to head home now. I'm pretty tired," I say. It's pretty much true, but I also don't want to tread on their horny toes. It's pretty obvious that they're gagging to bang each other's brains out.

"Of course, you're tired. You haven't had much sleep this weekend," Brianna says with a knowing grin. I blush profusely, but Michael suddenly gets back to seeing how far he can get his tongue down Brianna's throat. Geeez! I have to get out of here to make a hasty exit and no sooner have I closed the front door do I hear Brianna moaning in ecstasy. She's having the time of her life in there! I put my ear up to the door because I can't believe my ears but also curiosity has reared its ugly head. It becomes too much when I hear one loud scream.

"You fucking love it, don't you?" Michael says in a strained voice. I jump back from the door, and my cheeks burn with embarrassment at listening in on my best friend getting jiggy with her fella. I run downstairs, and my heated face welcomes the cool outside air. I get into Anthea and blast the air con to the point that it drowns out the radio.

I head home shocked at myself but also at how erotic Brianna and Michael sounded. Is that what Raphael and I sound like? Soon, I'm home. I park up Anthea and dash into my apartment block. I get to my floor and freeze. The sight that greets me is a tremendous one. Raphael is leaning against my front door with his eyes to the ground. They snap up to mine as I walk over to him. We don't utter a word but just gaze at each other. His hands cup my face, and he leans in to kiss me. I drop my bag so I can get my hands on him. They settle on his rock-hard chest, just his shirt separating us. I can feel the coolness of his skin through the material as his tongue licks at mine. A soft groan escapes his throat, and he reluctantly pulls away from me and drops his hands. His eyes open to reveal slightly cloudy pupils as he smiles a crooked smile at me.

"I thought I would stop by but found you were out. I was just about to leave when I heard your car," he says snaking his arms around my waist.

"I was helping Brianna move in with Michael," I say tilting my head to the side.

"Michael?" he asks, surprised.

"Yeah. He's her new boyfriend." I smile.

"She is hideous," he says with conviction. I pull a face of disbelief but can't help the smile creeping in. Not because I agree with him, but because of the way he said it.

"She was beautiful before, but now she's gorgeous. She's undergone quite a transformation. She's pretty slim and has bright red hair now," I say.

"This Michael must be blind or desperate," he scoffs.

"He's pretty good looking actually. They're quite taken with each other. I left just in time. The sexual tension between those two was almost tangible. I almost got a full-on show. As soon as I shut the door, I could hear their cries of *passion*. It was pretty steamy. I would be surprised if it didn't turn the whole block on," I say in a rush. Raphael raises an eyebrow at me. "Yeah, it was *that* steamy." I laugh. I break away from him and push him out of the way with my hand so I can open the door. I know that if I manage to move him, it's because he's let me, but I still feel great satisfaction in moving a vampire out of my way. He follows me in, and Marmalade runs straight to Raphael's feet, purring her little head off. "Wow, she really seems to like you," I say in surprise.

"Let me guess. You thought cats would dislike vampires?" he asks wryly.

"Well, yes. Creature of darkness and all," I say shrugging my shoulders and heading over to the couch. He closes the door and has sat before I get to it.

"How prejudiced of you," he says with a scowl, but I can see the humour in his eyes. "We are not creatures of darkness, and we are not hated by animals. Except Reggie. Everything hates him, even his wife," he says with a slight smile. His arms stretch out for me, but I step back so I'm playfully out of his reach.

"Why are you here?" I ask almost suspiciously.

"Do not even try to act like you would prefer I was not here," he says suddenly standing inches from me. I stare at the man in front of me, forgetting what's hidden beneath the surface. The things that he makes me feel are almost indescribable. A sense of complete fulfilment would be one way to describe it, at a push. Contentment at its finest. Something clicks in my brain, and before I can control it, my mouth is already opening. "Where is Nicholas?" I ask suddenly, breaking the moment between Raphael and me. His features momentarily show pain. A flash of vulnerability. But it's gone in an instant.

"He is in Chile with a group of vampire therapists," he says, his voice small. Whatever happened between them appears to run deep. I saw a glimpse of Raphael's agony, a dark chasm I don't want to see again. "I've got to get back. I have things to sort out," he says. His mind is clearly occupied by some trouble. I hope I didn't just set him off. He pecks me on my lips, and then he's gone.

CHAPTER TWELVE

Raphael

Abandoning Rosannah, I head back home. I had intended to stay with her, but when she mentioned Nicholas, it sideswiped me. Being with Rosannah feels so natural for me, it is exactly why I am here. So many humans wander this big wide world wondering why they are here. Questioning what they should do with the time they have. Vampires can wonder the same thing but have forever to think it over. I am fortunate to know why I am here, and what I should be doing, but I feel treacherous for it. I feel like I have stabbed my brother in the back even though I spotted Rosannah first. I may be a monster in many ways, and I may not be the best brother, but I do love my family.

Evangeline and Lawrence are in when I arrive home, and I can hear their argument before I even run through the open gates. They stop arguing as soon as I enter the house. Lawrence walks over to me looking like thunder, and Evangeline disappears, brushing past my shoulder on her way out and leaving the front door open behind her.

"What was that all about?" I ask Lawrence, closing the door.

"She's only gone and got the bloody Synod involved again. She can't help but meddle," he says clearly annoyed.

"She has involved them again?" I ask incredulously.

"It's not too bad this time. They only know about Alex. I didn't tell her that you visited Rosannah because she can't keep her big mouth shut," he says.

"What did The Synod have to say?" I ask him curiously. They can kill Alex, for all I care, but I would like to find out whom he answers to first.

"They're not too fussed, to be honest, but they think you've failed at sorting him out," he says shrugging his shoulders.

"There is no harm done then," I say with a slight scowl.

"No, but every time there's a new development, Evangeline goes running to them blabbing," he says, his shoulders slouching.

"As much as it annoys me, she is doing what she thinks is best. You know that she is not very bright. We have already lost one sibling. We do not want to lose another," I say with a sigh. We both snap our eyes to the door when we hear a car driving down the drive. A frantic heartbeat leaps out of the car and heads for the front door. I open it to see a panicked Rosannah. What in the hell has happened?

CHAPTER THIRTEEN

Rosannah

My head was in a spin and needed clearing after Raphael left. I decide to head out to the local shop to pick up a small bottle of wine. A few glasses with a nice hot candlelit bath is exactly what I need. I feel awful for making Raphael run. I had no idea how upset he was over his brother's departure. Chile, hey? Vampire therapists? Vampires must be in every walk of life. Hidden in every conceivable role that exists. With Raphael confirming where Nicholas is I can now put the idea of him being Michael to rest. Maybe doppelgangers do exist.

I arrive at the shop and look at all of the bottles of wine. I'm not a wine connoisseur, and I have no idea what is good or not by name. I simply grab a well-priced white wine and buy it. I walk out of the shop and the sight of a pair of butt cheeks mooning the night's sky stops me. They are peeping out from under a *very* short dress. Could they belong to Cindy? Surely not, there's no reason for her to be here. Besides, the last time I saw her was at Raphael's house when The Synod had a meeting. She's Vladimir's other half if my memory serves me correct. I chuckle to myself as I remember that she mooned the whole room countless times, and Lawrence had a field day.

I look around and see people gawking at the woman bent over in front of me as she fiddles with her huge killer heels. Some guy even honks his horn while hanging out of his window, drooling like a dog. This woman is completely oblivious, and I feel outraged for her. I rush over to her, intent on trying to restore some of her dignity, but she stands back up quite flustered. She shuffles off with tiny steps.

"Cindy," I call after her, hoping it's really her. The woman stops and turns around to face me. Her irritated face instantly lights up, and her eyes sparkle with recognition. It *is* her! She scoots over to me with a huge smile on her face.

"Rosannah," she sings as she air kisses my cheeks. "How are you?" she asks tilting her head to the side.

"I'm great. Oh hey, I've just bought this for a night in by myself, but you're more than welcome to join me if you'd like," I say with a half-smile.

"Ah. I'd love to," she squeals. Linking with my arm, we make our way to my apartment as fast as her little shuffles will allow us. It takes some work, but with a joint effort, we get her up the stairs to my front door. Once inside, Cindy takes off her gigantic heels. Why couldn't she have taken them off outside? Oh, that's right, the floor is dirty outside. I grab two glasses from my kitchen and bring them over to the table. I crack open the bottle and fill our glasses. Handing one to Cindy, who's already sat on my couch, I sit next to her.

"How are you holding up?" she asks, her voice full of concern.

"Erm, fine," I say. Why wouldn't I be? Unless she's referring to my *separation* from Raphael.

"It's so sad that Raphael had to throw you out. Who would have guessed Nicholas was in love with you?" She giggles, taking a sip from her wine. I suddenly feel sick. That's why they were arguing, and he attacked Raphael? Nicholas was in love with me. He knew that I had slept with Raphael.

"Everything's okay now," I say trying to smile.

"Has Nicholas come back then?" she asks. "I thought he was going to be in Chile for a while," she says with a frown.

"No, he's still there. I was referring to Raphael and me," I say, suddenly no longer wanting my wine.

"Oh well, that's great," she takes another sip. "Oh, I have the best news," she chirps. "Vladimir and I have set a date." She smiles.

"You're getting married? Oh, that's wonderful." I smile.

"Oh no, not that, silly. Vlad is changing me." She smiles. Should I be offended that she just called me that?

"Oh right, that's wonderful." I try to smile.

"He's going to kill me in two weeks' time." She grins. Kill her? Of course, to change someone into a vampire, they must die in the process. I try to hide my horror.

"If you don't mind me asking, why would you want to be a vampire?" I ask her.

"Vlad and I love each other and want to be together forever," she says dreamily.

"How does something like that even happen?" I ask, genuinely interested.

"Well, we had to meet certain criteria, and then we had to get a pardon from The Synod," she says in an excited rush.

"Criteria?" I ask intrigued.

"Yeah. They have to make sure that you really do want to be together forever. They did a brainwashing interrogation on me to see if all my answers were honest," she says.

"What about Vlad," I ask slightly confused.

"If a vampire says they want to be with a human forever, then it's accepted that they mean it. Vampires are indestructible, and there's nothing worse than being stuck with someone you hate forever." She laughs. *Of course.* That's very twisted, but it makes logical sense.

"So you're really willing to go through the change?" I ask amazed.

"Of course. Aren't you?" she asks surprised. That's quite an assumption.

"No," I answer simply. She blinks at me a few times in disbelief.

"No?" she asks, her voice small.

"Let's not talk about that. Let's talk about your special day," I say forcing another smile. She beams at me and launches into every detail. I sit and listen to it all the while trying to look excited for her. It will be a wedding-style event with Vladimir in a tailored black suit and her in a wedding dress. A dress that I've been roped into helping her find Mathias will be at the ceremony to officiate, and there will be a reception-style party a few days later. Photographs will be taken so that they can look back on their special occasion. It's all pretty disturbing, and I find it very sad that no one will be there for her at her changing ceremony. No parents, no family, no friends. They can't know at all.

"You've barely touched your wine," she says with a giggle. I actually haven't drunk any of it. My mind feels scrambled, and I'm quite glad when she stands up to leave. "I would love for you to be there for my transformation." She smiles.

"Err…" I don't know what to say.

"Oh, how wonderful. You'll be the only one there for me. Well, apart from Vlad." She grins. I force a smile at her. "Don't forget the fitting for my dress is Wednesday six pm sharp. I will hand you your invite then. I was holding off handing it out as it's addressed to you and Raphael, and I didn't want to write another one out," she chirps as she clambers into her skyscraper heels. She air kisses me and heads for the stairs. She takes her heels off this time. Maybe she's seen sense! I close and lock the door as I see her disappear down the stairs. I slump back onto the couch wondering what in the hell just happened. Two hours ago, I was meant to be having a relaxing candlelit bubble bath, and now, I've been nominated to go wedding dress shopping. A dress for what is essentially a murder that I will be attending! Well, that's what it is, isn't it? A murder. And the most disturbing thing about all of this? She's actually *happy* about it. And what about Nicholas? I have to know what happened. I need to talk to someone about this. Sadly, I can't talk to Raphael, so who? Ah, I know who. I run downstairs and race to Raphael's place in Anthea. The gate is already open, and I drive up to the house. My heart is pounding, and I'm worried about Raphael's reaction. Getting out of Anthea, I lock her and head to the door. It's opened before I can knock on that beast of a knocker. Worry flashes across Raphael's face.

"Is Lawrence there?" I ask. Disappointment spreads across his features. With his eyes fixed on mine, he pushes the door open to reveal Lawrence, who's looking confused. I signal for him to come over to me, to which Raphael growls. I shoot him an apologetic smile, and Lawrence is with me in a split second. I walk off towards Anthea and signal him to follow. He's by my car as I reach it. I unlock her, and he hops in. I look at Raphael as I open my door. He looks so confused. I get in and start her up. Driving off, I look in my rearview mirror. He's still standing there watching.

"You want to tell me what's going on?" Lawrence says wryly next to me.

"I'll tell you once I get home," I say, my eyes flicking to his quickly. He raises an eyebrow at me, but I ignore him.

Once we get back to mine, we head upstairs and enter my flat.

"Nice," he says, looking around the front room. I walk to the couch, and he's sat there instantly. I stop in my tracks, and he smiles at me. "Come on," he teases tapping the seat next to him. I let out a little laugh and go and sit next to him. "This must be quite important because you've dragged me all the way over here much to Raphael's chagrin." He smirks.

"I couldn't risk Raphael listening," I say guiltily.

"Must be serious then," he says feigning worry. I suck in a deep breath.

"I want to talk about Nicholas," I say in a rush. Lawrence's face drops slightly, but he quickly regains his usual grin.

"What do you want to know?" he asks, his voice serious.

"Why he fell out with Raphael," I say with hope.

"There's not much to say," he says getting up and walking over to the windows.

"I know that Nicholas is in love with me," I say. My voice is barely a whisper, but I know full well that Lawrence can hear me. He turns and his look is questioning. His eyes probing me.

"How do you know that?" he asks me suspiciously.

"I bumped into Cindy," I say and half-smile at him.

"Of course. Vladimir tells her everything," he says.

"As it should be with any couple who's deeply in love and very serious," I say. Lawrence is sat next to me in a flash. He wars with himself for a moment before he speaks.

"We didn't know until that morning. I mean we had an inkling that he fancied you from the dancing incident, but as far as we were concerned, Nicholas was having fun with our bets and his feelings weren't serious. That morning, I had teased Raphael as I usually do. Raph was the gentleman, not wanting to divulge anything, leading Nicholas and me to believe that he still hadn't taken advantage of being on his own with you," he says with a small smile.

"Raphael was a gentleman?" I ask feeling a sense of pride.

"Oh, yes. When it comes to you, he is, and that morning was no exception. He was impeccable. Stating that whether you two had slept together was none of my business," he says with a big grin. The smile drops as an unpleasant thought enters his mind, and he continues. "That's when Nicholas spoke up. He claimed it was his business and then declared his love for you. We all really had no idea. He'd kept the secret well. Nicholas provoked Raphael by stating that he would declare his love for you, and you would essentially go running to him. Raphael then revealed that you two had already slept together. Evangeline and I were shocked, but Nicholas didn't believe him. But then, as it dawned on him, he went insane. That's when you came downstairs," he says frowning.

"Vampires arguing are a little hard to ignore," I say with a small smile. "I'll take you back," I say standing up.

"I can get back just fine," Lawrence says with a smirk.

"Of course." I giggle. He walks over to the door and stops once he's opened it.

"I'm glad you're back in Raphael's world," he says with his back to me. I suck in a deep breath, and he's gone.

CHAPTER FOURTEEN

Raphael

Where in the hell are they going? What could Rosannah possibly want with Lawrence? Jealousy bubbles up inside of me, and I run out to the garden with the intention of following them. My phone starts ringing, and that stops me from chasing after them. I look at the screen and see that it is Mathias. "Yes," I answer the phone.

"Raphael, there are some things that need discussing. Are you available?" he asks. There is an urgency to his voice. I really do not want to see him right now, but it is my duty to see what he wants. I will get whatever it is out of Lawrence later.

"Yes," I answer deadpan and head back into my home. The phone line goes dead, and within five minutes, I can hear Mathias approaching the house. I open the door in time for him to race through. He dashes into the dining room, and I follow. I find him sat at the head of the dining table. The audacity of his actions offends me, and I hold back a growl. "What is this all about?" I ask, annoyed at how comfortable he is.

"We know that you have seen Rosannah," he says looking concerned.

"How do you even know about that?" I ask incredulously.

"That is of no concern," he says.

"It was Evangeline, was it not?" I ask. My sister's heart is in the right place, but it is sure annoying that she cannot keep her mouth shut. Though I wonder how it is she knows. She must have listened in without any of us knowing.

"She is not the only source of our information," he answers. This is typical of Mathias, acting as if he is in control when he is far from it. Something flashes behind his eyes and his expression hardens. "You should have notified me yourself, "he says quietly. This is true. With my dedication to duty, I should have. I honestly hoped I could keep this from The Synod, but with vampire ears everywhere and a sister who is intent on getting into The Synod ranks, keeping secrets appears to be a very difficult task. Mathias is now looking at me expectantly.

"In all honesty, I have been busy," I say. Mathias nods slowly as he reads between the lines. "What is happening with Alex?" he asks.

"I take it you know that he is working for a vampire and completely brainwashed into not remembering a thing?" I ask with a raised eyebrow.

"We are aware," he says carefully.

"Then you should also be aware that it is best to keep an eye on him until he has led us to whom he may be working for, and this means, in turn, keeping an eye on Rosannah," I say with calculation.

"You're playing a very dangerous game. If she decides to tell anyone..."

"She will not tell anybody," I say cutting him off.

"I will allow you to conduct this your way because it looks like you have things under control, but you must keep me updated," he says in a rush. I nod in agreement. "I don't mean to interfere, but it is my duty to tell you what is of concern to The Synod," he says with a soft voice. The Synod? We both know full well who he means. I walk off leaving him sat there before I say anything that I may regret. "Another thing," he calls after me. "Can you ask that sister of yours to stop calling us every five minutes with trivial things? I can only hold Reggie back for so long." I am at him in a split second.

"Since when does everyone answer to REGIUS?" I scream at him. Mathias blinks his shock away.

"You know that The Synod does not condone Reggie's beliefs, and I must point out that he has made no actions on his words," he says straightening himself up.

"If he were destructible, then I would have wiped him out by now!" I yell at him. This does not have any effect on Mathias. It is well known in the vampire world that Reggie and I would kill each other in a split second if it were possible. "If Reggie ever acts upon his *beliefs,* I can assure you that all Hell will have to pay. If Hades exists, I will personally deliver Reggie to him and spend the rest of my eternity gladly watching him suffer!" I say through gritted teeth. The threat hangs thick in the air. I watch as Mathias's eyes register it. It is a small while before Mathias speaks up.

"Are you aware that Rosannah is being invited to Vladimir's ceremony?" he asks.

"I have no idea what you are talking about," I answer honestly. He pulls a face that would suggest he questions my statement but goes on to tell me.

"Cindy is going through the transition. Vladimir is changing her," he says. Ah, so Rosannah must have told Cindy she saw me, and Cindy told Vladimir in

101

turn. Goodness knows what *I saw Raphael* turned into once the news reached Mathias.

"I was not aware of this at all. This is my jurisdiction, not anybody else's," I complain. "Who agreed that Vladimir could do this?" I ask.

"We tried to reach you several times over the last month, but you were somewhat indisposed. The decision fell to me, and I ruled in favour," he says looking slightly embarrassed.

"Oh, right. I see," I say as awkwardness falls between us. "So when is Cindy's ceremony?" I ask tucking my hands behind my back and rocking back on my heels.

"Not this Wednesday but the following one. Then the revealing will be on Saturday," he says.

"Oh, okay." I half smile.

"I think I shall go now that I've addressed all that needed to be discussed. I will leave Rosannah and Alex in your hands. I trust you will take care of any problems that may arise. Both of Cindy's ceremonies will be at Vladimir's, but I'm sure there's an invitation floating around somewhere." He smiles and then he is gone.

I have been around for hundreds of years and minutes normally fly by, but the twenty minutes it takes for Lawrence to arrive back after Mathias leaves are torturous. It feels like it has been forever when Lawrence finally bursts through the door. Without saying a single word, he goes into the kitchen, gets himself a glass of blood, and sits at the breakfast bar as if nothing has happened. I walk over to him and stare at him incredulously as he sips and murmurs in appreciation. Very slowly, mid-sip, he turns to look at me.

"What?" he asks innocently. I growl at him, and half a smile appears on his face.

"What did Rosannah want?" I ask, feeling surprisingly desperate to know.

"Just stuff." He shrugs.

"Do not play with me," I warn.

"Raphael. It's not something you're really going to want to know about," he says with concern. I shoot him a look, and he looks at the ceiling shaking his head. His eyes flick back to mine.

"She wanted to talk about Nicholas," he says, and I cannot help but wince at my brother's name. We stay in silence, neither one of us sure what to say. After a while, I decide to break it.

"Vladimir is changing Cindy." I smile.

"Really? So there's going to be a party?" he asks with a smirk.

"It would seem so," I say.

"Panty Strangler," he says with a huge grin spread across his face.

CHAPTER FIFTEEN

Rosannah

With nothing happening since having that talk with Lawrence, and Raphael keeping his distance, Wednesday evening comes around very slowly.

When I walk into the dress shop, I find myself slightly nervous. Cindy is buying a wedding dress for the wrong reason, but I don't get to dwell on that thought for long when a very happy lady greets me.

"Hello. I'm Julie. Is there anything I can help you with?" She grins at me.

"She's with me, and you can stop that chirpy nonsense. We can look through the dresses ourselves," a voice rings out behind me. I watch as Julie shrinks and slinks away. I turn in surprise to see that the voice of authority belongs to Cindy. She shuffles over to me and air kisses my cheeks. "Hey, sweetie." She smiles and leads me to a rack of dresses. She then spends the next three hours trying on dresses. Silk, satin, lace, cream, white, pink. You name it—Cindy tries it on. Poor Julie tried once to interject, but Cindy bit her head off. I wouldn't have thought Cindy could be like that, but she's actually a bit scary with an underlying menace to her. Eventually, after a marathon of trying on dresses, Cindy comes to a decision.

"I think I'm definitely going for the dark cerise one." She smiles.

"Which one?" I ask. She's tried on at least three dark cerise dresses.

"The one with all the lace layers." I know the one. It has a plain silk corset top and a bouffant of lace skirts. "Now it's your turn." She sits down on one of the low backless hard cushioned chairs.

"What?" I ask, panicking.

"Go on," she encourages, pointing over to a rack of dresses. I shoot a quick glance at Julie, but she ducks behind the counter. What made you even think she would save you?

I end up trying on a variety of garish numbers much to Cindy's amusement. Eventually, she puts me out of my misery.

"I'm going to pay for my dress. I'll meet you at the register." She laughs. I'm glad one of us found this amusing, not. Julie gives me a pleading expression as I enter the changing cubicle. Sorry love, I have to get changed. You'll only be with Cindy for five minutes.

When I finish, I emerge to an interesting scene. Cindy is in full swing talking about Vladimir, and Julie looks like she just wants the ground to open up and swallow her whole. I walk over to them as Cindy pays a frightened Julie.

"Your dress will be ready to collect in a week," she says, her voice faltering. Cindy smiles sweetly at her, and we head out of the shop. Expecting this to be the last time I see her until her special day, I bid her farewell, but she walks with me to my car.

I unlock Anthea, and Cindy looks at me expectantly.

"Do you want a lift?" I ask her.

"To yours? That would be great." She smiles and gets in the passenger side. *Okay.* I get in and head home.

TANIQUELLE TULIPANO

Cindy attempts to climb the stairs in her killer heels.

"Didn't you take them off when you left here last time?" I ask.

"Oh, yeah." She smiles and takes them off.

Once in the flat, Cindy sits down on the couch.

"Would you like a drink?" I ask.

"I'll have tea. No milk or sugar. I'm watching my weight," she says with a smile. Not that Cindy needs to lose any, but how much weight does she think she can lose in a week? Brianna managed loads, didn't she? Maybe Cindy will too, but I don't really agree with it. I make her tea and take it to her.

She sits in silence for a while, drinking it and stroking Marmalade, who has perched next to her on the armrest.

"Everything okay?" I ask.

"Well, no. Not really." She pouts.

"What's wrong?" I ask, not really wanting to know.

"I think I might be getting cold feet," she says, her bottom lip quivering slightly.

"Why?" I ask, suddenly caring.

"It's such a big step to take. How will I know if Vlad will still love me in a thousand years' time?" she asks with tears threatening to spill down her cheeks.

"It certainly is a very big step, but *Vlad* has been around for a long time..."

"Two thousand, five hundred, and forty-eight years," she says, interrupting me. I can't hide my shock; that's pretty old.

"I like older men," she says dreamily.

"Well, he's been around long enough to know whether or not he wants to spend forever with you," I say with a smile. She stares at me for a moment. I start to worry that I've upset her when she suddenly throws her arms around me.

"Oh, you're so clever. I knew you'd make me feel better," she squeals in my ear.

"There, there," I say as I pat lightly on her back. She pulls back with a huge smile on her face and releases me.

"Oh, while I remember," she says as she digs into her handbag. "There you go. You're invited to both ceremonies." She smiles.

"Thank you," I say taking the light pink envelope from her.

"Also, if you could just say a few words at the ceremony, that would be great," she says catching me completely off guard.

"What?" is all I can manage to say.

"You know, a poem or song. Something beautiful." She swoons as she gets up.

"I'm not too sure I can do that," I say trying to get out of it. Cindy takes her cup to the sink and then puts her heels back on.

"You will be fine. I can't thank you enough." She grins. Looks like I'm definitely doing a reading.

Ring. The doorbell rings, startling Marmalade. Please tell me it's not Alex. I race over to the door and open it. A smile plays out across my face at the sight of Raphael. I hear a shuffling behind me and turn to see Cindy making her way over to me.

"Hi, Raphael," she squeaks.

"Hi, Cindy," he greets her. She shuffles out of the door and turns to face me. Throwing her arms around me, she hugs me tight.

"Thank you so much, Rosannah. I know you'll do great. I'm going to go now. Lord knows I'm in need of some really hot vampire sex," she gushes. I look at Raphael, who is trying not to laugh.

"Bye, Raphael," she says happily as she turns and shuffles away. Raphael's eyes are fixed on mine as I start to step back from the door. He watches as I keep going until I reach the other side of the room. He pushes the door with his right hand, and it slams shut behind him as he stalks slowly forward.

"I saw you today," he says with a half-smile. My heart sinks.

"You did?" I ask, my voice small.

"I spotted what appeared to be you in a wedding dress. I have to admit I had to take a double look just to be sure," he says.

"Cindy's idea, not mine," I say.

"Ah, that would explain the garish choices then," he says knowingly. I have never really thought about marriage, but suddenly, I'm wondering what Raphael's thoughts are on the subject.

"What do you think of marriage?" I ask.

"I have only thought about it once," he says carefully as he stops.

"Emily?" I ask. He nods in reply. "What do you think of it now?" I press on.

"After Emily, I never gave it any more thought. I had no reason to, but if I think of it now, it does not appeal to me. I can *live* forever, so I certainly do not need the law to show others that one is mine. In hundreds of years from now, a marriage certificate will mean literally nothing," he says with a smile. He looks at me and his face drops. "Ah, females love weddings do they not?" he asks.

"Some do but not me. I've blocked it out. My mother is determined for me to marry only to divorce," I say.

"Excuse me?" he asks.

"My mother wants me to find a rich man, marry him and then divorce him to take all his money in the process," I say feeling incredibly embarrassed.

"Does your mother not believe in love?" he asks. The subject of love makes me very uncomfortable.

"No, she doesn't. I had an interesting day with Cindy," I say trying to change the subject.

"She seemed very happy when she left. What did you help her with?" he asks with his eyes smouldering as he continues his way over to me.

"She was getting cold feet about her transition," I say, watching him.

"And you helped her with that?" he asks tilting his head to the side, surprise spreading across his face.

"I've just convinced Cindy that it's okay to let Vladimir murder her and that it wouldn't be a huge mistake," I say as I realise how twisted that sounds. Raphael is up against me instantly, looking down at me.

"Is that what you think? "he asks. His voice is a low tremor, and his eyebrows knit in confusion.

"What else would you call it?" I laugh in disbelief. He doesn't answer but stares, as if he's trying to figure me out. After a time, he leans down and plants a kiss on my lips.

"I do not know what I would call it," he says looking into my eyes. After his lips touched mine, I no longer care.

"No talking, just kissing," I say as I pull his lips back to mine.

CHAPTER SIXTEEN

Raphael

Discussing weddings and marriage with Rosannah was a week ago and that time has gone by faster than I would have liked. I have been quite apprehensive about taking Rosannah to Vladimir and Cindy's *ceremony*. She has already expressed horror about it, and she has good reason. No part of a transition is nice to witness. There are three stages in the process. The first is the introduction of vampire blood into the human body. This is a task that has to be done very, very quickly due of the rate in which vampire skin and flesh heals itself. There is not much to see during this part for humans, but vampires can see exactly what is going on.

The second stage is dying. Even though it can take mere minutes, this is by far the most traumatic to witness and frightening to experience. As the vampire blood spreads through the human body, it shuts down organs and bodily systems on its way. When the vampire blood hits the brain, it preserves it so that memories and personality are not lost. It also ensures that the human does not stay dead. This stage then finishes with shutting down the brain.

The third and final stage is the transformation itself. Even though the body is technically dead, the vampire blood is not. It gets hard at work to change the body from human to vampire. The first thing it does is switch the brain back on, so to speak, so you have to experience the full effects without being able to move. It is an incredibly painful and gruelling experience, physically changing every molecule in the body, strengthening and hardening skin, bone, and muscle while shrinking internal organs. This stage can take anywhere from a few hours to a few days. It depends on the age of the vampire the blood comes from. The older the vampire, the faster the change.

Rosannah will be there for two of these stages, and it is bad enough that she views it as murder. There was a time not long ago when I would have delighted in watching Rosannah's reaction, but now it will not bring me any kind of happiness.

After the transformation is complete, Rosannah will be amazed, and it may just change her overall opinion.

Now I find myself staring at the mirror in my bedroom. I am staring into the eyes of a man who has not aged a day in over two hundred years. Only a shell of the man he once was remains.

"You're looking very dapper," Lawrence says popping his head into my room. I feel incredibly sorry for him. Half of him is missing and yet he puts on a brave face. He could hate me as I helped to drive Nicholas away, but he does not.

"When the occasion calls for it." I turn to him smiling.

"Are you looking forward to it?" Lawrence asks with a smile.

"Yes," I say trying to appear enthusiastic.

"You don't sound too happy about it," he says walking over to me.

"I have... reservations," I say reluctantly.

"Why would you be concerned?" he asks.

"I do not think it is a good idea for Rosannah to watch Cindy die. I am worried about how she may react," I say. "Are you aware that she thinks turning a human into a vampire is an act of murder?" I ask, my brow knitting.

"Murder?" he asks in surprise.

"Unequivocally, I might add," I say.

"That's a bit strong, isn't it? "he asks in disbelief.

"Her words, Lawrence, not mine," I say with a frown.

"I suppose it depends on the circumstances. If it's against a person's will," he says.

"They come back to life so to speak and are given immortality," I reply.

"Does that matter to Rosannah? He asks.

"It appears not," I reply.

"Why on earth is she going then?" he asks confused.

"I think she feels obligated to go. Cindy has no family or friends attending and latched on to her. Perhaps she does not want to turn her down for fear of upsetting her." I shrug.

"Oh man, I don't know what to say to that," Lawrence says with a grim smile.

"It's not fair that I'm only invited to the revealing party," Evangeline cuts in. She's standing in my bedroom doorway having just made her way there. Lawrence and I turn to face her to see that she is sulking and holding a pink piece of folded paper.

"Think about it. You now have more time to plan your outfit for Saturday," I say hoping she will take the bait.

"I didn't think of that!" she exclaims and scurries off. So predictable.

"Don't worry, Raph. It'll be fine," Lawrence says clapping a hand on my shoulder. I smile and hope that he is right.

I race down to my car and head over to Rosannah's. I head up to her floor and ring the bell. I smile as I hear her racing heart moving toward the front door. She opens the door, and I stand there staring at her. I look at her from head to toe, my eyes lapping her up. She looks stunning. The colour of her dress is striking against her pale skin; her hair tousled up to expose her delicate neck. I am hard instantly, and it takes all of my strength not to have her naked and take her where she stands. She smiles innocently at me. She is quite oblivious to the extent of craziness she drives me to. I will have to tell her when the time is right.

"Ready?" I ask.

"Yes." She smiles.

CHAPTER SEVENTEEN

Rosannah

Before I know it, the time to get ready for Cindy's ceremony is here. I've been quiet most of today. Brianna picked up on it but put it down to my *mystery man*. If only she knew the truth. And what is the truth? I'm reading a poem out in front of a group of vampires. I'm then to witness one of those vampires kill his human girlfriend because they love each other and want to spend eternity together. I'm sure there's meant to be something romantic in that, but it's just sick and grotesque to me. I couldn't make it up if I tried, but I'd be happier if I had made it all up.

Once I've had a shower, I throw my dress on. I spent ages deciding on this particular dress. It's bright coral and a 50's style prom dress that comes down to just above my knees. It's silk and has layers of petticoats underneath. I've had it for some time. My mother bought it for me in hopes that I'd attract a man. If only she knew I was wearing the man catcher dress to go out with a man, well, vampire. I cringe at the thought. I've never been brave enough to wear it before now. I'm a bit of a wallflower; I like to sit in the background and not the limelight. Unless it's karaoke, then I'm up there like a shot.

I don't know why today seems like the perfect day to wear this dress, but what does someone wear to a murder? I clip my hair up in a loose chignon and sit.

While I wait for Raphael to pick me up, I have a quick look at the poem I've chosen to read. I have loved this poem since I first read it. It's by an unknown poet. It's dark, exquisitely beautiful, and so fitting for Cindy and Vladimir's love. *Ring*. My heart leaps; Raphael must be here. I put the poem in my bag, and I try to casually walk to the door, even though deep down I want to rush and yank it open. I've been longing to see Raphael for days. I open the door, and the sight of Raphael in his suit is enough to make me moist. He stares at me; his eyes take on a darker shade as they skim up and down my body.

"Ready?" he asks with a crooked smile.

"Yes," I reply, and we walk arm in arm down the stairs and outside.

"So you have a car then?" I ask with a little laugh as we walk up to a Mercedes.

"I have three." He smirks as he leads me to the passenger side and opens the door for me. I slip in and sink down into the low seat as he closes the door. He's next to me in an instant and starts the car up.

"How long will it take to get to Vladimir's?" I ask.

"With my driving, about an hour," he says. Just as I'm about to protest, he puts his foot down, and we speed off.

The journey to Vladimir's is a long but fast one. We drive down many winding country lanes. It's pitch black everywhere except for our headlights and a few small lights in the car. I watch as the scenery goes by but glance every so often at Raphael. Watching him drive is so damn sexy, and I can't help but quietly moan every time I look at his hand and thigh resting on the gear stick and floor.

I look up at his face and see his jaw is clenched.

"If you do not stop moaning like that, I will pull over and fuck you senseless," he says through gritted teeth, his eyes dead ahead. *Geeez.* I slap my hand over my mouth to stop a yelp from escaping.

After a while of watching the dark scenery whizzing by, I feel like I need to say something.

"Raphael, aren't you driving a bit too fast?" I ask. He looks at me and raises an eyebrow. "What if someone is coming the other way or an animal jumps out in front of the car?" I say trying to justify myself. He's still looking at me. "Watch the road," I almost yell.

"I am a vampire with super sensitive hearing and quick reflexes," he says gripping the steering wheel tighter. I look at his hands and suck in a breath. "Don't you dare," he warns just as I'm about to moan again.

Eventually, some lights appear in the distance. Soon, we turn off the road and drive down a gravel lane to approach them. The headlights highlight a tall private fence alongsideus, and we eventually come to a large Victorian-style house. It's all one storey, and as we park up, I can see that it's built out of lashing of small red faded bricks. Huge stone windows adorn the front, and I can't help but feel impressed. No sooner has Raphael cut the engine that he's opening my door. I watch as Raphael's eyes drop slightly and turn darker. A low growl escapes his throat. I look down to see what has drawn his attention. I've forgotten I'm wearing a dress and that I'm in a low car. I've stuck a leg out causing my dress to raise a little. I jump out quickly and flick the skirt down. I don't risk looking at Raphael. I know his black eyes will be on display, and if we keep going like this, we won't make the ceremony. I walk as quickly as I can into Vladimir's house as the huge front door is already open. Raphael catches me up instantly. We are greeted by a very smiley...*butler*?

"Welcome, straight through there." He smiles, all teeth, signalling to a room to my left. We walk into a cosy dark grey room with low lighting, and the scene that greets us is a bizarre one. There are chairs set up on either side of the room, like a wedding but with just one row. I can see that the males are on the right, and the females are on the left. Mathias and Vladimir are stood at the top of the room. They both look like they're missing from a funeral. All that's missing are the coffins.

Everyone except Reggie turns to look at us with pleasant faces. I force a smile at them all and go over to the seats on the female side. There are three seats to spare, but I take the outer most one. The only vampire I'm happy to sit next to here is Raphael. I expect him to go and sit with Reggie and Porticus, but he stands against the far wall next to Vladimir. Why is he over there?

"Now that we are all here we can start." Mathias addresses us all with a smile. Looking at his odd face, something clicks in my head, and I remember something that Raphael told me. He said that Mathias had replaced parts of himself with other body parts, but vampires are meant to be indestructible. How does that work? Quite simply put, it doesn't. Either way, Raphael must be lying. Either Mathias is not made up of different things or vampires are not indestructible. I will have to ask Raphael later.

Music starts playing, distracting me from my thoughts. It's a piano piece I don't recognise at first, but as it gets into the song, I realise what it is. It's "Tongue Tied" from Red Dwarf. I bite my lip to stop myself from laughing, but I do have to admit this piano version is quite beautiful. I glance at Raphael, who's looking at me with a raised questioning eyebrow. I smile at him, shake my head slightly, and look over my shoulder to see Cindy making her way to Vladimir dressed in the dark cerise wedding dress that she bought last week. She looks stunning in it, and I'm almost sucked into the whole wedding theme. She reaches Vladimir, who looks visibly upset. No tears, though, of course, which reminds me quite poignantly why I'm actually here. Cindy stops next to him and tries to console him with a hand on his shoulder. It does nothing to calm him, but he places a hand over hers.

"You have all been asked here to witness the start of this transition," says Mathias, addressing us all once again. "Now, Vladimir I must ask that you do understand what you are doing and are certain that you want to do this?" he asks turning to him.

"Yes," Vladimir replies.

"And Cindy, you know what it is you're partaking in?"Mathias asks Cindy.

"I do," she squeaks. I can't help but wonder if she knows what partake¬ means. How judgemental, I feel a little ashamed at the thought, but she's not the brightest spark. Mathias then turns to Raphael.

"Raphael, you are here to see that the correct procedure is carried out and will stop the ceremony if anything is not adhered to. Is this correct?" he asks. Oh, so that's why he's standing over there. I forgot he was in charge of the changing of humans.

"Yes," Raphael replies, his eyes flicking to mine. How many transitions has Raphael authenticated? Witnessed even? This is getting weirder by the minute.

"Now for a reading from Rosannah," Mathias says as he looks at me and smiles. I pull the poem out of my bag and walk to the front of the room. Mathias moves to the side, and Cindy and Vladimir go and sit down. I give a nervous smile to the light grey eyes before me. Reggie sneers, and I glare back at him. It causes him to look away, thank goodness. I clear my throat and look at everyone.

"This is a poem from an unknown author. It's called 'The Unknown World.' It seems very fitting." My brows knit, and I look down at the page and read.

"The deep wounds would weep, and the hearts
would cry
Forever out of reach, the river of life ran dry
Time stood still and yet years passed by
A dim flame burned alone, the darkness knew why
The recess threatened, the crevasses overflowed
A forbidden territory, its secrets unknown
A nightmare alive, the horrors it showed
Some made of flesh, others of bone
The edges were frayed and the plane unfed
Of all the worlds needed, this one was dead
Venture was sought, a foot did tread

The euphoria was bleak, and the end was ahead
Broken one lays, the dream was torn
A lesson learnt, a lesson we morn
A tale we hate but have to perform
To all the masses yet to be born
Eventually a spark, a ray of hope
Easier to swallow, hard to choke
The shackles are off, and now one is free
Together we dance for all eternity."

Pulling my eyes back up from the paper, I'm faced with curious and inquisitive looks. Reggie is busy looking at his nails, the tart that he is, but everyone else looks riveted. Cindy looks astounded. I have no idea if she understood any of it. I look over at Raphael, who is expressionless. Blank, empty. *What the...*

"Thank you, Rosannah. You may sit back down," Mathias whispers to me, pulling me from my thoughts and causing me to jump. I hadn't noticed that he was right next to me. Why would I notice? He makes no sound. I nervously stumble back to my seat and try to mentally prepare myself for what I know is coming. A storm is brewing, and I have no idea if I can ride it out.

"Now the couple would like to say their vows," Mathias says signalling Vladimir and Cindy to join him. Vows? Cindy certainly is going all out with this *wedding-themed murder*. A chill shoots down my spine at the thought, and I involuntarily look at Raphael. He looks concerned, but I dismiss it with a shake of my head. Vladimir and Cindy stand side on to the rest of us. He takes her hands in his, and I watch as his eyes take on a darker shade. Wow, is he...horny?

"Cindy," he says, his voice cracking with emotion. I then realise that the dark eyes can signal strong emotion, too. I want to look at Raphael again, but I also want to listen to the vows. "My love, I am so thankful to have you, and nothing will make me happier than to have you forever. I am honoured to be the one to change you," he says with a slight tremble. Is that it? Is that all he has to say? He looked like he was going to go all Shakespearian or something. I could see the emotion—he truly loves her—but the words were... lacking, I suppose. Cindy seems to love it. I can't see her face, but I can hear her high-pitched sobs. Her cries sound like a little puppy's bark or a squeaky toy.

"Vlad. I loved you from the first moment I saw you. I had never thought about living forever before I met you, but now that we're together, I want nothing more than to be yours, forever. I'm glad that you are the one turning me," she says between squeaks. Vladimir smiles a huge a smile.

"Well, there's nothing left to say other than you may bite the girl," Mathias says with a grin.

"Are you ready?" Vladimir asks Cindy. She takes a deep breath.

"Yes," she replies. Low music starts to play, and I recognise the song straight away. It's one that I really like. Well, not anymore with this memory now attached to it. It's "One Last Breath" by Creed.

CHAPTER EIGTEEN

Raphael

Standing here and listening to this drivel is not what I consider to be a wonderful thing. It has only just started, but it is enough to almost bore me to death. This is complete and utter nonsense. The whole idea is a sham. A wedding theme? Before long, anyone granted a transition will want the convenience of a drive-thru. I refuse point blank to entertain the idea. I have not authenticated many transitions, but the ones that I have were better than this. One was a silent one with no words spoken—just bite, die, and move on. That is how it should be done although there was one full of the most romantic and emotional speeches I have ever heard.

As disdainful as I find this particular ceremony, I do have to admit that the couple does certainly love each other. But how does one know they want to spend eternity together? I have been around for a while, and in that time, I have grown incredibly tiresome of my own family, so how would love fair?

"Raphael, you are here to oversee the procedure and will stop the ceremony if anything is unsatisfactory. Is this correct?" Mathias asks pulling me back into the room. Nothing about this is satisfactory, but I cannot halt a transition purely based on the fact that I find it distasteful and somewhat tacky.

"Yes," I say, my eyes landing on Rosannah. She has no idea how divine she looks in that dress.

"Now for a reading from Rosannah," Mathias says as he walks over and stands next to me.

I watch as Rosannah fumbles with her bag to find a piece of paper and then walks warily to the head of the room. She smiles courteously to everyone, but Reggie sneers at her. I have to use all my control not to go over to him and punch him in his smug mouth. Not that it would do any damage, but it would be the equivalent of an extremely offensive insult. I feel great satisfaction when Rosannah glares at him. He has the decency to look away, albeit with the tiniest bit of shame. I still think my idea was better.

"This is a poem from an unknown author. It's called 'The Unknown World.' It seems very fitting," she says looking unsure. As the words of the poem flow from her, I stand rooted to the floor. I am mesmerised by the words. There is such depth to them with layer upon layer of meaning nestled in amongst them. Rosannah's voice is small but full of conviction. She commands every word as if they are her very own. Once she is finished, I scan the room. All eyes are on her, and no one looks disappointed except Reggie, who is not paying any attention. He delivers what is expected of him.

Blondie is a sobbing wreck, and my eyes return to Rosannah. Why did she pick such a poem? It has so many different ways of interpretation. She catches me off guard staring at her and her brows knit in confusion. Mathias leaves my side and is next to Rosannah before she even realises.

"Thank you, Rosannah. You may sit back down," Mathias says, startling her. She practically staggers back to her chair with nerves and embarrassment.

"Now the couple would like to say their vows," Mathias says motioning for them to stand up. I inwardly sigh. There really is no need for all of this. I hear Rosannah take in a deep breath, and I look at her with worry. She shakes her head to indicate that she is fine and then looks at Vladimir and Blondie.

"Cindy," Vladimir almost sobs. Suck it up, man!

"My love, I am so thankful to have you, and nothing will make me happier than to have you forever. I am honoured to be the one to change you," he says with more conviction. His emotion is in abundance, but it is a shame the contents of what he just said let him down. I thought there was more depth to Vladimir. He looks at Blondie expectantly who takes longer than necessary to realise it is her turn.

"Vlad. I loved you from the first moment I saw you. I had never thought about living forever before I met you, but now that we're together, I want nothing more than to be yours, forever. I'm glad that you are the one turning me. I wouldn't let anyone else sink their fangs into me. You know I'm not that kind of girl," Blondie says with sickeningly high-pitched sobs.

"Well, there's nothing left to say other than you may bite the girl," Mathias says with a smile. I nervously look at Rosannah, but she looks fine.

"You ready?" Vladimir asks Blondie.

"Yes," she squeaks. A song starts to play that I have never heard before, and I wish never to hear again. This is not my kind of music at all. I do not mind heavy guitar music or sweet melodic classical music, but definitely not sentimental rubbish. I watch as Vladimir very expertly bites Blondie, then his own wrist, and quickly places his wound to hers. The blood transfer is complete, and Vladimir's wrist heals before his arm reaches his side after he has dropped it from her neck. Blondie goes through the normal motions of a transition. The usual commotion that accompanies *dying*. I smile lightly and then realise that the only normal heartbeat in the room is racing. A strange thing starts to happen to me. A knot of anxiety ties its way around my chest. I look at Rosannah, and the sight of her hits me harder than anything has ever hit me before.

CHAPTER NINETEEN

Rosannah

In the blink of an eye, two wounds appear on the side of Cindy's neck facing us. A trail of blood seeps out of them and trickles down, finally reaching the top of her dress. An emotional smile spreads across Vladimir's face. Cindy turns to face us and a big smile plays on her face. She looks perfectly fine. She even giggles. The transition looks like it's gone smoothly, and I can't help but match Cindy's smile. Suddenly, fear spreads across her face, and her pupils dilate. Black threatens to swallow the light blue. I can't fathom the horrors that are playing out behind those eyes. Her face screws up, and she lets out the most hideous tortured sound that causes me to wince. Mathias steps back and Vladimir captures Cindy with his hands. As he lowers her to the ground, he cries waterless tears. I watch helplessly as Cindy begins to thrash about and scream. My stomach knots and the room begins to bear down on me. With a huge weight on my shoulders, I shrink in my chair and almost pool onto the floor. The heat escapes my face, and tears sting my eyes. My vision becomes tunnelled, and all I can see is Cindy.

She begins to gasp for breath, and it becomes unbearable to watch. I feel physically ill. She takes a final breath and stills. I have to leave. I slink off my chair to the left, and while bent over, I stagger to the door. Thankfully, it's open. I race outside to a nearby bush and my stomach spasms causing hot bile to burn its way up my throat and out of my mouth. Raphael is suddenly next to me and reaches out to grab me. I slap him away, and our hands battle it out beside me as my stomach churns again. All the muscles in my throat spasm painfully as more bile comes up.

"Jesus, Rosannah!" Raphael exclaims. After a few more painful heaves, my stomach is empty. I stand up and wipe my mouth with the back of my hand. Raphael reaches out to me. The sight of him fills me with horror, and I jerk away from him.

"I can't believe I came here!" I exclaim.

"Rosannah, it was just a little blood that is all," he soothes as he steps closer.

"Just a little blood?" My voice hits new highs and cracks under the strain. "It was unequivocally murder!" I shout, but the strain of trying too hard means it is nothing more than a fiery whisper but the intention hits home. Raphael looks almost appalled.

"Do you think that I was murdered?" he whispers in disbelief.

"Yes," I say incredulously. He stares at me astounded.

"Rosannah, what happened to me was a long time ago," he says stepping forward, encroaching on my personal space again. What?

"This has nothing to do with you. This is about what I was so unfortunate to have just witnessed. God Raphael, doesn't anything ever affect you? Move you? *Scare* you even?" I ask, my voice only just managing to work. A strange expression spreads across Raphael's face, but in an instant, it's gone, and he's reaching for me again. Jumping back involuntarily, I push his cool hands away. "I don't want any vampires anywhere near me, especially you. You all make me feel sick," I say as my stomach twinges.

"You do not mean that," he says visibly wounded.

"Oh, I definitely do," I warn.

"Rosannah," he pleads, but then something changes behind those eyes, and I suddenly feel exposed. How in the world am I going to get away from one of the fastest creatures on the entire planet?

CHAPTER TWENTY

Raphael

Wait, why am I pandering to this? Pleading with her? I can take full control of this situation and of her. I am a creature of darkness; I must be true to myself. A sense of determination falls over me. Rosannah's face, which has gained the shade of rage, pales with fright. Her subconscious commands her arms to wrap around her torso as if that will save her from me. I stalk forward.

"What are you doing?" she asks with a tone of terror.

"You will not spurn me," I command, creeping in deliberation. Herding her like a lost lamb towards my car.

"Are you trying to brainwash me?" she asks in disbelief.

"No, I am not! I am simply instructing you," I say as I reach her. "You will get in the car, and I will drive you home," I say with conviction. Resistance flashes across her face, and I watch as she turns and runs towards the gate. For goodness' sake, this woman is not thinking straight. She knows how fast I am, but I let her run. Not to let her go but to save our audience from an abduction-style charade in front of Vladimir's home. I look at the main downstairs window, and I can see everyone, minus Vladimir and Blondie, staring at me through the net curtains.

"I thought that watching the blond woman dying would be a great show today, but this is better. Look at him staring at us in horror. What's the matter, Raphael? You look like a slapped arse!" Reggie yells. Mathias growls at him, but he laughs. I get in my car ignoring the others and focus on Rosannah. I can hear her running feet, racing heart, and heaving breaths. I decide to give her fifteen minutes. I know how far she is. I am thankful the others inside do not emerge, but while the others stopped looking, Reggie has stayed and continues to laugh.

When the time is up, I start the engine and head off in Rosannah's direction. She is still running, and I can see her in the distance. I pull over, and within seconds, I have left the car, grabbed my target, and returned. Rosannah is buckled in before she knows what has hit her. She looks bewildered. How can she possibly be so surprised?

"I told you that I will drive you home," I say almost gloating.

"Where do you get off on telling me what to do?" she asks with raised eyebrows. I set off at a breakneck speed.

"Now, we both know what gets me off, and it is not simple idle instructions," I say with my eyes dead ahead, an instant hard-on making itself known. Rosannah gasps and lets out a small moan. "Not this again," I groan.

I drive back in record time, but the journey is a torturous one.

I have had a hard-on that would not abate, and the only thing that got a good seeing to was the accelerator.

I pull into my drive much to Rosannah's surprise.

"I thought you were taking me home?" she asks in confusion.

"Change of plans," I say as I pull up to the house. I can see the garage is open, and my other two cars are there. It means that Evangeline is in. Instant erection deflation. It is amazing that Evangeline insisted on borrowing both of the cars; she has her own, as does Lawrence, but they have always wanted to use my things. I turn the car off, racing around and opening Rosannah's before she has even undone her seatbelt. She gets out of the car with a scowl on her face and almost stomps her way to the front door, which opens before she gets there.

"Hey," Lawrence smiles. Great, he is here, too.

"Move,"Rosannah demands.

"That's not the usual greeting I get when I've been missed," Lawrence says as he sidesteps and lets Rosannah past. "You know what? We can catch up another time," he says after her. Flashing me a grin, he races out of the door. One down, one to go. I walk into the house, and Evangeline confronts me next.

"I don't know what you've done, but she's not happy," she says accusingly.

"Did it not occur to you that I may not have been the one who upset her? The sight of Lawrence's face alone is enough to provoke anger," I say with raised eyebrows.

"Oooooooh," she says and stands there looking into space. After a short time of this, I clear my throat in an attempt to snap her out of it. "Oh, I'll be off then." She smiles, and she too is gone, shutting the door behind her. Now that my siblings have gone, I close my eyes and listen to the heartbeat drumming in

Rosannah's chest. She has retreated to *her room*. I race up there to see her standing by the left window, staring out into nothing. I have the ability to see what is out there regardless of how dark it is, but Rosannah's human eyes cannot cope with such lack of light, so this could be an indication that she is planning to ignore me. I make myself known with slow, deliberate steps that cause the floorboards to creak. I can sense Rosannah's hostility, and instantly, I am behind her. Not touching but close enough to feel the crackle of electricity that flows so abundantly between us. I lean to her ear.

"Is this all still about the transition? I know it was not the most wonderful of things to witness, but I have seen *much* worse," I whisper pulling her hair back to expose her succulent neck. A strange sound vibrates through her chest, almost feline-like. Unfortunately, not a purr. She deftly moves out of the way, and once again, I am left hanging. She gracefully glides over to the other window and turns on me with a mixture of anger and confusion on her face.

"Yeah, you see things like today all the time. Blood, gasping for breath, fear. I don't. I've never seen or heard anything so disturbing in my life, and the fact that you attempt to be sensitive about it only with me is insulting. Not to mention that you've brought me here to...have your end away no doubt. I saw good in you, saw you as a man rather than a vampire, but at every step, you painfully remind me that you're a monster. A cold-hearted, evil creature of darkness. The epitome of nightmares. The very foundation of all that is wrong in the world, "she says with surprising calm. I cannot control myself, and I am at her instantly.

CHAPTER TWENTY-ONE

Rosannah

He is in front of me in an instant. His eyes pitch black.

"Ask me again," he says through gritted teeth.

"Ask you what?" I ask flinching away from him. He's going to bite me; I can feel it. The last thing I need is Raphael biting me into oblivion when I'm meant to be angry right now. I prod the thought away with a sharp stick.

"The question you asked me earlier," he says looking down at me. "Ask me it again," he says slowly.

"It was a rhetorical question, Raphael," I try to reason.

"Ask me it again!" he shouts. I gasp at the ferocity of his voice. I'm so shocked by his aggression that I stand there silent and motionless. He closes his eyes and appears to be calming himself down. "Please, "he begs, his brow furrowing. He opens his eyes, and they are now a simmering dark grey. "Ask me the question again," he whispers. As realisation dawns on me, my heart begins to pound, and I'm gripped by fear. Almost paralysed by the thought of the answer I might get.

"Doesn't anything move..." I start. Raphael slowly shaking his head stops me. I take a deep breath and try again. "Doesn't anything scare you?" I whisper, barely able to get the words out. Raphael puts his forehead on mine and squeezes his eyes closed.

"Yes," he whispers. "The possibility that you do not love me is unbearable, and it scares me to death," he says as if in agony. He stands back up and looks at me with jet black eyes. Tormented and expectant. I'm so in love with him, it's beyond belief, but my mouth can't formulate the words he so desperately wants to hear. After a short while, he turns around and walks off, leaving me standing there in shocked silence. I don't hear where he went, but I wander to his bedroom. It's empty, no Raphael. I'm about to leave when the scent of the room hits me. I look at the bed and go and sink into it. Emotions warring inside of me, I have no idea if I should cry or try to get myself off with the scent overpowering me. I opt for a different option. I tear myself away and go to look for him.

I find him in the TV room. The TV is on, but the sound is off. Light softly flickers across his face, and it's enough for me to see how upset he is. My heart aches at the sight, but Raphael won't look at me. I walk over to him. I climb up and straddle his lap, putting his face into a slight shadow. His face doesn't change, but I can feel him swell instantly against my moist panties. He reaches up and runs his hands up my back. I whimper at the contact and ride his lap, rubbing myself against his rock-hard length. God, I *need* him, as deep inside of me as I can get him. He suddenly grabs my wrists and looks deep into my eyes. All I can see is a tortured soul. In a split second, he has me on the floor on my back, his hips between my thighs. He's grinding hard against tender nerves,

136

right where I need it. I cry out and feel myself quicken. Suddenly, he growls and sits back on his knees. That tortured look is on his face again. I sit up and reach for him, but he's gone in a split-second. I'm left high but certainly not dry. Irritated, I get up and head upstairs to his room. He's here this time. With his back to me, his head hangs low. His left arm is clutching the nearest poster at the foot of the bed, and the other is fist down on the bedspread. It looks as if these are the only things holding him up.

"Raphael, what did I do wrong?" I ask. He lets out a little cynical laugh and turns to face me with a peculiar smile.

"That is the funny thing," he says as the smile slides from his face, replaced with a grimace. "You have not done anything wrong," he says in a dark tone as he falls back to sit on the bed.

"What is it then?" I ask perplexed. He's in front of me in an instant, and I yelp from being startled.

"You do not get it do you? Not in the slightest," he says. His wild eyes and vicious tone have me retreating, backing out of his bedroom slowly. He follows me at the same pace while his stare bores into me. My eyes widen when I feel the banister at the small of my back. When Raphael reaches me, he puts a hand on the rail oneither side of me and traps me like a defenceless animal cornered by a predator. I would lash out, but my common sense tells me it would be entirely futile. I swallow hard and dig deep for my voice.

"Don't get what?" I ask with a tremble. I inwardly curse myself for showing how frightened I am. He reaches out and runs a thumb down my cheek. Is he...*trembling*?

"I want you," he hisses out, the strain evident on his face.

"You have me." I half-smile trying to defuse the tension. He slowly shakes his head.

"It is not enough," he whispers. My brow knits in confusion.

"What more can I possibly give you?" I ask as desire slowly rises in me with his thumb bushing softly up and down my cheek.

"I have your mind. I have your body," he says then his eyes drop to my chest. "But I do not have your soul," he says with pain etched across his face. I freeze up. This is too much to deal with. I can feel myself cringing at how open and raw he is right now. How open and raw I feel. My fear rises and douses out any desire that was building up. I'm petrified, and all I want to do is run. Raphael looks into my eyes and must sense what I'm about to do because his grip tightens on the rail. I can hear the sound of his bare hands crushing it. I have no idea where I'm going to go or how I am going to get away from Raphael, but I stupidly duck beneath one of his arms and start toward the stairs. A hand grabs my wrist and spins me around, and I'm faced with a pissed off Raphael. "Do not dare walk away from me!" he booms. My eyes fall to the banister. There are deep indentations in it from his hands. The very hand that grips my wrist did half of that! I start to pull my hand wanting to free it. If I could have detached it and left it there just to get away from him, then I would have.

"Oh, but it's okay for you to walk away from me?" I ask sarcastically. His face twists slightly, and I stop struggling.

"I am pouring my heart and soul out to you. Can you not see that I am in love with you?" he pleads. Geeez! Panic hits me, and I start to struggle again. "Why are you trying to run?" he asks, his grip showing no sign of letting up.

"Because I'm petrified," I say as my eyes start to sting. I try with all of my might to wriggle free, but his grip tightens painfully.

"Ahh!" I cry.

"Why?!" Raphael demands, and the last of my resolve disintegrates.

"Because I love you, too." I sob. "My God, I'm so in love with you it hurts!" I say as tears cascade down my face. He pulls me into his rock-hard chest, and his lips clash with mine. Our lips are frantic, and the kiss is painful. He pulls back, scoops me up in his arms, taking me to his room, and lays me down on his bed. His eyes are as black as the night, his face taut and his jaw hard. He doesn't say anything as he strips off his clothes, leaving them where they land. He makes his way over to me, and my eyes rake over his nakedness, landing on his rock-hard erection. He's going to fuck me into the next world, and I moisten and throb at the thought.

I should be running for the hills; instead, I get up and peel off my dress. Raphael moans at the sight of me in just my panties. This dress is fortunately very padded so no bra is necessary.

I hook my thumbs under the elastic of my panties and slip them off. I feel the cool air hit my slickness.

Raphael growls. He's suddenly pulling me tight against his body so we are chest to chest. He starts trailing kisses along my neck, causing my skin to prickle with goosebumps. Without warning, he suddenly spins me around and plunges his fangs into my hypersensitive neck. I cry out as he latches on and sucks. A hand snakes its way down to my waist and splays across my stomach, holding me in place. Sucking gently, he lightly growls and finishes up with a lick of his tongue. He turns me back to face him.

"Get on the bed," he says, his voice strained. Following his command, I scramble up onto his bed. "Lay on your back and open your legs," he all but whispers. I shamelessly obey and watch as he climbs on top of me. He lowers over me, and I can feel his erection pressing against my opening. Grabbing my wrists, he pins me down, and a groan escapes my throat. "I have wanted to hold you down and fuck you in my bed since I first saw you," he growls and slams into me. We both cry out. Unable to control himself, he sets a fast pace. The thrashing against my cervix pushes me over the edge so quickly it takes me by surprise. It causes every muscle in my body to spasm. Raphael quickly follows, growling out his climax as he grinds unforgiving into me. Eventually, Raphael's pace slows down, but he continues to make love to me for the rest of the night.

In the morning when I wake, I'm glad and relieved to find Raphael still wrapped around me. I go to get up, and he growls in protest but lets me slip from his arms. I slip my dress and panties back on, and I head back to my room. Looking around, it's the same as I left it. I have a quick shower and throw on my normal attire of a vest and jeans. When I head downstairs to make myself some breakfast, a peculiar sight greets me. Raphael is at the hob cooking.

"Take a seat." He smiles playfully. A few minutes later, he serves up a full English breakfast.

"You actually cooked me breakfast?" I ask with a giggle.

"Do not look so surprised. I am capable of many things. Cooking is one of them." He smiles sitting opposite me. It makes me wonder just what else he's good at doing. I already know one thing he's incredible at doing. Before my thoughts get the better of me, I dig into my breakfast, and it tastes so good. I look at Raphael whose smile fades and is replaced with a blank expression. "Rosannah," he starts. "Are you going to the revealing party? "he asks warily. My stomach twinges at me, and I shake my head. "The revealing will not be anything like yesterday. Blondie will be like me. She will not be in any pain," he says with a warm smile. Blondie? I feel a little bit better, but I'm still not convinced. Raphael is using the future tense, which means that she's still suffering. "It will be a huge celebration, and I shall be there with you. If you get there and you are not comfortable once you have seen her, then we can leave," he says with a grin. I really should go to see if she's okay. I would like to remove the last sight of her from my mind, and this I really hope will work.

"Okay, I'll go," I say, holding my hands up in surrender. Raphael looks very relieved, and I finish up my breakfast in silence. Once I'm finished, Raphael whisks my plate away and washes it up. My thoughts turn back to Cindy and I have to know something. "Raphael?" I ask staring at the floor.

"Yes?" he answers.

"Was yesterday what it was like for you? I mean did you go through the same sensations? The same actions?" I ask, keeping my eyes on the floor.

"Yes, essentially. Although, the situation surrounding my transition was a lot different," he says, his voice low. I look up at him and see his expression is sombre.

"I don't understand. Why would anyone want to go through the transition?" I ask.

"Some people want forever," he says, his brow knitting.

"Why would anyone want forever?" I ask. Oh great, now I sound like a child. Why this, why that. He looks at me with an expression so intense it scares me.

CHAPTER TWENTY-TWO

Raphael

"Some want to stay young, some to live forever, while others do it for love," I say. I do not want to think about forever with or without Rosannah. Her brow furrows, and her face goes from fear to...determination.

"Something doesn't make any sense to me," she says putting her hands on her hips. Why does this make me feel uneasy? "You told me that vampires are indestructible," she says.

"That is correct. It is a concept that may be difficult to understand because humans can be damaged so easily, but vampires really are indestructible," I confirm.

"What about Mathias? How can he be made of different bits if he's indestructible?" she asks. Oh, damn. I made the colossal mistake of opening my mouth the day I told her about him. I half smile at her, but her face turns stony. She is not going to let this be. In a split second, I grab her and make straight for the crypt. Shutting the door behind us, I head to the end of an aisle. Rosannah is stunned but her stern expression returns.

"What I am about to tell you must never, and I mean never, be repeated to anyone. Not even me. You do not know who could be listening," I say in a rush. "I am about to divulge the biggest secret in the vampire world," I say in a hushed voice. Her face softens. "Mathias is the first," I say reluctantly.

"The first?" she asks in confusion. Then it hits her. "He's the first ever vampire? How did that happen?" she asks with amazement.

"I was not exactly forthcoming about how old he is," I say.

"He's older than two thousand years? Just how old can he possibly be?" she asks.

"He is seven thousand years old," I say. Rosannah's eyebrows shoot up. Being around for seven thousand years is difficult for even me to comprehend.

"How did he become a vampire if he was the first one? Surely he wasn't born like it?" Rosannah asks incredulously.

"Well, sort of. Mathias was born without a name. He was only referred to as Ma. He was very pale and thin. His family believed he was sick and would die, but death never came. He ate normal food but hated it because there was something he wanted more. Since he first saw it, he longed to drink human blood, and he got the opportunity to when he was fifteen. A freak accident left a family member dead, and the fresh blood was too tempting for Ma. After he had filled his belly, he knew that he needed blood to flourish. He started to kill people to be able to drink their blood, but it did not take long for his family to find out the truth. They banished him out into the wild, and after roaming aimlessly, he eventually came across another man who, just like him, was pale and liked to drink blood. They came to an agreement that they would live together but would not drink blood from each other. For many years, they lived and survived on animal blood until Ma's companion died of old age. Ma did not have much time left on this Earth and mourned his loss terribly. It did not stop him from feasting on his comrade, leaving just bones. It was not much long after he had buried the remains that he felt a change. He had incredible strength and no longer felt his age. He felt it was divine intervention to help him seek revenge on the family that threw him out."

"Most of the family and villagers he had once known had died, but that did not stop him. Like a tornado, he tore through the village that was once his home. He punished its residents by cutting his arms deeply and forcing some to drink his blood while the others watched. When he was done, he killed everyone and left their bodies where they fell. Ma was amazed at how quickly his arm healed afterwards and without a mark or scar. With all the people dead, he now had an entire village at his disposal. He moved back into the village, but things were not as they seemed. Soon some of the dead awoke, and it did not take him long to realise that they were the ones he'd forced to drink his blood. He had wondered how far his healing abilities went and so he decided to experiment on those who had risen from the dead. Chopping bits of them off, he put them back on to see what and how fast things healed. He quickly discovered that everything re-joined except the head. That is when he had the idea to keep creating others like him but in a cleansing way. He thought that if he and the others could heal then, maybe he could eventually have ones that could not be killed."

"Out of the initial ones that came back, he killed all but one. He got that one to create another two and then killed the creator. He then attempted to kill one of the two, and he succeeded. Then he got the remaining one to create another two, killing the creator afterwards. He continued until he ended up with two indestructible creations. He told them to create more, and then he disappeared," I say.

"That doesn't explain the different body parts and how he can't find his original ones," Rosannah points out.

"After he disappeared, he changed the skin on his head and neck. He altered his voice and lived as a different person for some time before he took on the name Mathias and returned. I was only joking when I said he had changed his body parts and that he did not know where the original parts were," I say with a chuckle.

"I don't find the joke remotely funny, you know. What happened to his original head and neck skin?" she asks with a wrinkled nose.

"The skin rotted away thousands of years ago. He will never look as he did, but it does not bother him. He is used to it now," I say.

"So was it Mathias who called his creations vampires?" Rosannah asks.

"No, it was the human race that eventually came up with the name vampire for creatures similar to ourselves. Unbeknownst to them, we really existed and continue to exist. And unbeknownst to any living creature with the exception of you, Mathias, and me, Mathias is the one who created the vampire and that, collected with the knowledge that Mathias can be killed, is very dangerous," I say looking at

Rosannah's shocked face. After a moment's silence, Rosannah speaks.

"Can't a normal vampire bite him and make him indestructible?" she asks.

"No other vampire apart from me would ever think of attempting to put Mathias intoa transition, and as it stands, he is happy with how things are. Everything about him is the same as the rest of us with the exception that extreme force can remove his limbs. Again, this is something that no vampire would try deliberately because they all assume he is indestructible. It is not how I have advised him to exist as vampires can still be extremely violent toward each other. It only takes one very annoyed vampire to attack him with full strength in the wrong way and reveal his secret or actually kill him. But, alas, he will not listen to me. We have no idea what would happen if I attempted to put him into the transition, and he simply is too frightened to find out," I say.

"So, he's quite stubborn then. Do you know who the first two indestructible vampires were?" she asks me.

"Regius and Porticus," I say with a smile.

"But they're much younger than Mathias," she exclaims.

"It took a few thousand years to finally create indestructible vampires. It did not happen overnight," I say incredulously. Her eyes narrow once more.

"So vampires get punished for unlawfully killing or changing humans?" she asks.

"Yes," I say, wondering where this is going.

"And vampires with the exception of Mathias are indestructible?" she asks.

"I thought I told you not to mention that!" I shout.

"Just answer the question," she says with annoyance.

"Yes," I growl.

"So tell me, Raphael, how do you punish indestructible vampires? "she asks hands on her hips. Oh, you think you have caught me out telling lies?

"The only thing we can do," I say shrugging my shoulders.

"And what's that?" she asks with a smug smile.

"Eject them into space," I say. Ha! That wiped the smile off her face. I walk off leaving her there dumbfounded. I am halfway up the stairs when she catches up with me.

"How in the world do you eject a vampire into *space*?" she asks, following me out of the crypt entrance.

"With *great* difficulty." I smile.

"Oh come on, how is that a punishment? It doesn't kill them, does it?" She laughs. I stop and turn to her.

"Does it not? Think about it. A creature doomed to float for eternity through a never-ending space. No food, no companions, no way back home. If they are lucky, then they may land on a planet! Now, if that does not kill them inside, I do not know what will! "I growl. She looks startled, but she recovers quickly.

"What about black holes or stars?" she asks.

"No vampire that has been ejected into space has ever made it back to tell us what they have experienced out there. And we couldn't travel out there just to drop a naughty vampire into a black hole to see what would happen," I say with a half grin. Rosannah laughs but then turns serious again.

"So, how long have you been able to eject vampires into space?" she asks. I turn and carry on towards the house.

"We have only been doing it since man was able to travel into space. We did not have the technology until man did, so as soon as it was possible, we started ejecting vampires into space. It works well as there are some of us who do not deserve to remain here," I tell her.

"What did you do before?" Rosannah asks with wonder.

"There was no actual punishment we could give, but we threatened all sorts of crazy, untrue things. Being *cured* for one. That surprisingly worked because amazingly no one was brave enough to see if we could cure them. Believe it or not, there are some of us out there who like being the way we are," I say as we enter the house.

"Do you?" she asks, trying to hide the horror she so blatantly feels. I turn around and walk up to her so we are millimetres apart. Her heart starts to race, and her breathing becomes erratic. I lean forward so my lips are right by her ear.

"Yes," I whisper truthfully. A shudder rolls through her body, and she gasps. "Get your things together and I shall take you home," I say reluctantly.

CHAPTER TWENTY-THREE

Brianna

After a long day, all I want to do is snuggle up on the couch and cuddle. Michael is sat on the couch waiting for me when I get home as if he's read my mind.

"Sit," he commands simply. It's just a word, but what it evokes in me is something else. I take my jacket and shoes off and go sit next to him. His big burly arms wrap around me. "How was your day?" he asks as he plants a kiss on my forehead.

"It was okay, but Rosannah was very quiet today. Must be that mystery man of hers," I reply.

"That might be true, but to be honest, it's you who I wanted to hear about. Right, question time again," he says with a chuckle dropping his arms from me. We're having one of our *normal* moments because Lord knows how crazy our relationship is. I turn to look at him.

"Fire away," I say raising an eyebrow.

"Tell me about when you lost your virginity," he says, something lying behind those big brown eyes.

"That's not a question," I say with a small bite of sarcasm. He gives me a hot but stern look. I swear this man could make me do *anything* he wants. "Fine. I was seventeen, and it almost didn't happen," I say with a light giggle. "There was this house party that everyone was going to. I remember the look on my mum's face when I asked her if I could go. She looked a mixture of horror and anger. I stupidly told her that I would be going with Rosannah. It seemed like a good idea at the time especially when my mum's face melted into a smile. My mum thought that if Rosannah was going, then it must be a safe place. Rosannah was miss goody two-shoes. She always was and always will be."

"I realised my mistake when my mum insisted that Rosannah came over first before we headed to the party. I should have really just told her the truth. Instead, I decided to convince Rosannah. I had to beg upon beg Rosannah to come, and eventually, she agreed. I was ecstatic, but she wasn't too happy. My mum gave us a big speech about keeping an eye on each other and told us to be back by a certain time. At one point, I thought she was going to tell my mum the truth, but she didn't. Once at the party, it didn't take long before Rosannah and I separated. I tried to find her, but I got pretty drunk.

"There was this cute twenty-one-year-old guy who befriended me. I think his name was Chris. We went back to his place, and one thing led to another, and we ended up having sex on his couch. I really wanted it, but it was just awful and not how I imagined my first time would be. Although he took great care to be gentle, it still hurt and it sobered me up quickly. After the deed was done, he cuddled me for a while, but I just wanted out of there. I went to the bathroom and called Rosannah. She was still looking for me, and I felt so bad. I told her where I was, and she came and got me. I know she had an idea of what I had done, but she never let on. I never saw the guy again, and

Rosannah has never mentioned that evening since," I say, feeling a little embarrassed. "So, what about you?" I ask turning to completely face him.

"I was thirteen. I had gone down to the local river for a swim. A woman came along and began chatting to me. She was friendly enough and was very pretty. She couldn't believe I was so young and told me that I looked older than my age. With the promise of meeting her teenage daughter, I went back to her home. Once there, I soon found out that there was no daughter. The woman revealed that she wanted to sleep with me. She was fifteen years my senior, but it didn't stop me from fucking her. Once I was done, I ran off," he says with a smile. I try not to look horrified, but I can't help it.

"That's disturbing," I manage to get out.

"How is it so? It's just flesh rubbing flesh that results in the most wonderful conclusion," he says and laughs.

"What? It's paedophilia," I say in disbelief. He turns serious.

"Where I come from it's called a score!" he shouts.

"In this day and age, it's illegal wherever you're from!" I shout. Something flashes in his eyes and he stands up with his back to me. He must be pretty mad at me. I'm not going to argue with him about this. I know that what happened to him wasn't right, but I'm not going to push him away because of it. Maybe one day he'll let me help him understand that it was wrong, but I'm going to bury this information...for now.

"Please tell me the rest of the story," I beg. Michael's shoulders drop; he appears to let his anger go and sits back next to me. He smiles at me and carries on.

"My only experience of orgasms before then was masturbation, and after that day, I never masturbated again. That particular woman became what people call a fuck buddy for quite a few years," Michael says. This was worse than I had thought. I force a smile, and he carries on.

"I boasted to my brother about my first sexual engagement. He's three years older than I am, and he couldn't believe I'd had sex before him. He refused to believe it at first, but he noticed all the little changes that happened with me. I practically grew up overnight," he says looking deep into my eyes.

"You have a brother?" I ask with intrigue.

"Yes. Is it so hard to believe?" he asks with a cheeky grin.

"No, it's just that I could have set Rosannah up with him if I had known, but now she has someone." I smile.

"Well, my brother's taken anyway," he says with a grin.

"Will I get to meet him one day?" I ask.

"Yes. I'm planning on it soon," he says with a smile. After a while, his brow furrows. "Did you really mean what you said about the way I lost my virginity being disgusting?" he asks as his eyes run over my face. Oh God, I can't go down this route again; we'll end up fighting again. I grab his hands in mine.

"I'm really sorry, Michael. I was just jealous of the ones that have had you before me," I say with a half-smile. It's true; I am jealous—insanely jealous—but not about that sick woman. That has thoroughly pissed me off. Michael's face becomes serious again.

"You don't think I'm not jealous? That some scum had his pathetic excuse for a dick in you? I can't stand the fact that there have been other men out there who have even touched you! "he says with such aggression that it frightens me. My God, what has gotten into him? "How many have there been?" he demands. I stare at him, taken aback. "Well? How many?" he asks.

"Three," I whisper.

"What?" he yells.

"I said three," I say a little louder. He pulls his hands from mine and goes over to the window. I have no idea what to do. Should I go to him? Should I leave him alone? I get up to go to bed when he halts me with a command.

"Stop. Don't go anywhere," he says calmly but with authority. He turns to look at me. "I'm sorry, Bree. I can't help it." Coming over to me, he holds me at arm's length.

"I love you, "I say. With such a whirlwind going on inside of me, the words have slipped out of my mouth before I can stop them. He looks at me for a moment.

"I love you, too, "he says. He's finally said the words I've longed to hear. He pulls me close and starts to tear at my dress. I rip at his clothes too, and in no time, we've stripped each other naked. His mouth clashes with mine, and he sucks my bottom lip into his mouth. With a light bite, he causes me to yelp. It's such a turn-on. He groans as his teeth scrape along my lip until it pops out of his mouth. "Turn around," he commands, his voice thick with arousal. I do as he says, and he bends me over the couch arm, pushing my head down. The leather is cool against my burning cheek. I hear Michael growl at the sight of me completely exposed to him. I hear the tear of foil; my heart races, and I feel so exhilarated. "What do you want?" Michael asks with a strained voice. I want this man balls deep in me.

"I want you." I moan as he rubs the end of his cock up and down my wet folds. I've never needed anything so much in my whole life.

"You're so wet," he hisses. "Beg me," he commands through gritted teeth.

"Please, Michael. Please fuck me," I beg. He groans loudly as he buries himself deep in my pussy. We both yell out as he begins to move back and forth. Michael picks up the pace until it's painful. This isn't like anything we've done before. It's harsh and is over in a matter of seconds with him grinding and gritting his orgasm out. It doesn't make any sense; he always makes me come but not this time. He pulls out and walks off to the window again, and an awkward silence falls between us.

"Is everything okay?" I ask him nervously.

"How about dinner with us and Rosannah to celebrate our newly declared love?" he asks without turning around.

"Yeah, sure," I reply.

"Tell me the details once it's sorted," he says.

CHAPTER TWENTY-FOUR

Rosannah

Getting the time off work firstly to go to Cindy's *murder* and now for her revealing party was actually a lot easier than I thought. I knew I would have to stretch the truth, and it made me incredibly nervous. I hate lying, no matter what the situation is, and always feel as though it's obvious. Like I have the words 'I am a filthy liar' painted across my forehead. I stuck as close to the truth as possible.

"Marie, can I request a couple of days off work?" I had asked her as I handed her my holiday request form. She took the form and read it. Her face scrunched up a little. "They're quite random," Marie said. I didn't need to tell her anything, but I felt guilty for some reason.

"It's for a wedding ceremony and reception," I said in a rush.

"I thought these kinds of things happened all on the same day, "she pondered. Looking back, I can see how ignorant that actually was, but at the time, I had started to panic. I had no idea what to say, and my mind went blank. Fortunately, Marie saw some kind of sense. "I suppose all sorts of things happen these days and don't some religions have weddings that take a few days?" she asked. With a sigh of relief, I smiled at her and nodded. Marie then signed my form, took a copy of it, and handed it to me.

I didn't hear anything about it until the day after the first event. I had dreaded going into work that morning, and I was exhausted from lovemaking with Raphael. After arriving at work as the day went on, I thought I'd gotten out of telling my colleagues about the *wedding* I had been to the previous day. It was nearly home time when I was pounced on

"So, how was the wedding? I would have thought you'd have talked about it by now," Marie said with a warm smile. I suddenly felt sick.

"Um, it was okay," I said as I went into overdrive, shutting my PC and getting ready to go home.

"I bet the bride was beautiful," Marie said five minutes later.

"Eh, something like that. Bye," I said before I rushed out of the office with Brianna chasing after me.

It's now the day of Cindy's revealing party, and Raphael is driving us. Vladimir is hosting it at his mansion. Apparently, they wanted to keep it all at home. I'm pretty nervous, and Brianna hasn't made it any easier. I needed to try and relax as best I could earlier, but she came up to my apartment to tell me that Michael and she have declared their love for each other and asked me to go out to dinner with them to celebrate. Who does that? Getting engaged, yeah. Moving in, sure. But not declaring your undying love for each other. But at least this way we can have dinner the way we were meant to the first time I met Michael. I plan to rope Raphael in and turn Brianna's celebratory dinner into a double date. This is for two reasons. The first being that Brianna hasn't met Raphael yet—well, not that she remembers. And secondly, Raphael and I haven't had a proper date yet. I would have preferred our first one to be just us two, but I don't want to be the third wheel at Brianna's dinner. I have to be thankful to Brianna though because she lent me the dress I'm wearing. It's a black bodycon dress that hugs my body tightly. Raphael growled his approval of it. A simple 'you look nice' would have done, but that's not the way of the vampire apparently.

Raphael rests his hand on my knee as he speeds down the winding country lanes that lead to Vladimir's place. It takes a while, but before I know it, we're parking up. Raphael comes around and opens my door, holding his hand out to me as the gentleman he is. I remember to be more careful getting out this time and slide around, keeping my legs shut. Raphael takes me by the hand and pulls me gently from my seat but not without his eyes dropping.

"Not that I am complaining but why did you opt for a black dress?" he asks me as he locks the car and leads me to the front door.

"Normally, a party after someone has died is called a wake, and black is worn to it," I say with a tight smile. Raphael slowly shakes his head as we make our way to the front door.

We greet the butler with a smile, and I dig into my handbag to pull out our invite. I go to hand it to him, but he ignores it.

"Please make your way down the hall and enter the third room on the right," he says with a friendly smile. As we walk down the hall, I lean over to Raphael.

"How does he know we're meant to be here? He didn't even ask our names," I ask with a whisper.

"He's brainwashed to know who is allowed in," he whispers back.

"How is that even done?" I ask incredulously.

"He is made to remember who he has already seen, and then he is shown pictures of those he has not. Once he knows names and faces, he is then brainwashed to know who is actually invited and is allowed in," he says.

"Isn't that just long winded?" I ask with a sigh.

"It is the vampire way," he says with a shrug. I pull a face at him. "It has its advantages as well, you know. He can notify us about a party crasher before they get anywhere near the front door." He smiles.

"Oh," I say. I didn't think of it like that. We reach our destination, and I go to step over the threshold into unknown vampire territory when Raphael stops me with an arm around my waist.

"Are you ready for this?" he whispers in my ear. My breathing hitches, and my heart races. Being this close to him always puts me in a spin, especially when he's touching me.

"Yes." I breathe. His eyes darken, but he takes my hand and leads me into the room.

I'm amazed. It's huge and full of people. There's a dance floor in the middle of the room and round tables scattered around the perimeter. Black tablecloths decorate each table, and silver feathered and sparkly centrepiecessit neatly in the middle of each one. There's even a head table! Although there are many of them, the guests are quiet and subdued. They must be brainwashed. After a little while, music starts to blare out of the speakers without any warning and a spotlight focuses on a corner of the room.

"Now that you are all here, ladies and gentlemen, may I introduce to you the happy couple," a voice booms out over the speakers. I look at where the voice has come from and see a rather jolly man stood behind a DJ booth at the top of the dance floor. I look back to the highlighted doorway, and Vladimir appears with a brunette on his arm. Who the heck is that? Oh, my God, it's Cindy! She looks incredible. She's dressed in an elegant black ball gown, dark makeup and black hair. The sweetheart neckline of her gown confines her boobs well. Her skin is super pale, and her light grey eyes shine. "Right Here Waiting" by Richard Marx starts to play, and Vladimir and Cindy have their first dance. Once they have finished, a crowd gathers around them, and after saying a few polite words to them, Cindy spots me staring and gracefully makes her way over to me.

"How are you feeling?" I ask nervously as she reaches me.

"I feel fantastic. I've never felt better." She smiles.

"How beautiful does she look?" gushes Vladimir, who has just joined us.

"Cindy, you look amazing. The dark hair really suits you." I smile.

"It was all part of my *alter ego*," she says with hand quotations.

"Alter ego?" I ask.

"Growing up with huge boobs, it didn't matter what was in my brain because all people saw were those. Guys thought I must be easy, and girls thought I must be a bitch and would be after any man I could get my hands on. I got sick of the stereotype, but in the end, I thought that if I couldn't beat them, then I should join them, so to speak. I thought I'd give people something to actually talk about rather than have them making stuff up. I bleached my hair, made sure everything was on show and acted as I was expected to act, without all the sleeping around, though. Vladimir is my first and last," she says with a sigh. How sad and pathetic that people can be so judgemental and make a lovely person like Cindy feel like she had to change herself to satisfy stupid expectations. What makes this worse is the fact that it took her becoming a vampire for her to feel comfortable enough to be herself.

"I have many people to see. I shall see you later," she says and then glides off arm in arm with Vladimir. I turn to Raphael amazed.

"I told you that she would be fine," he says.

"I know, but all that stuff about not being able to be herself before is deeply upsetting. Looking at her now, it's nice to see that she is happy and at peace with herself," I say. Music starts to play again, and suddenly everyone rushes to the dance floor. What the hell is going on?

"What would you like to drink?" Raphael asks me.

"Oh, just a white wine if there's any. If not, then surprise me," I say. I think I could use a good drink or two to get me through this evening. Raphael gives me a cheeky grin and disappears into the throng of people packed on the dance floor.

I've been standing waiting for him for a while when a hand taps me on the shoulder. I jump and turn to see who it is. Piercing green eyes penetrate mine.

"Alex? What the hell are you doing here?" I ask in surprise.

"It's nice to see you, too." He laughs.

"Sorry, it's nice to see you, but this is the last place I thought I'd see you at," I say truthfully.

"Well, with it being my cousin's wedding reception, I would have thought I should be here." He laughs.

"Cindy's your cousin?" I ask.

"Yeah, she's my mum's sister's daughter," he says. He thinks for a moment before he speaks again. "Shouldn't I be asking you why you're here?" he asks. How on earth do I explain this one?

"Oh, I was invited by Cindy," I say.

"Cindy has never mentioned you before. How do you know her?" he asks. What is this?

"I met her through the groom." I grin. It's true I guess.

"Vladimir is quite the guy, isn't he?" Alex asks with a fond smile.

"Oh, yeah. He's great," I say with a forced smile. A light growl interrupts us. Raphael has appeared behind us and has walked between us. Putting an arm around my waist, he hands me a glass of white wine and smiles at Alex.

"What a nice surprise to see you here," Raphael says. Alex looks down at Raphael's territorial arm. A look of anger spreads across his face, and he looks like he's about to say something to Raphael, but another growl stops him. Alex gives us an uncomfortable smile and disappears back into the crowd. I look at Raphael, who appears to be gloating. Jealous much?

Not much happened after that for the first part of the party. There were no speeches, thank goodness, but hey, this isn't a real wedding. The whole thing, with the exception of Raphael's jealousy feast, is quite boring actually, and then Lawrence arrives. As soon as he walks in the door, the ladies flock to him like seagulls to a stray morsel of food. They peck and squawk at him, all desperate for him to throw them something, anything, and follow him when he heads to the DJ.

He says something to him and takes a microphone from him. With a light growl, the crowd backs off and leaves him in the middle of the dance floor. The music changes and a screen lowers from the ceiling. Soon Lawrence is singing and dancing, shaking and slapping his ass all over the place. The ladies are screaming in delight, and Lawrence is lapping it up. The song choice is very Lawrence, "I want to be your Lover" by Prince. When the song finishes, the women rush Lawrence, all wanting a piece of him. Well, all the females with the exception ofCindy, Evangeline, and me. She sneaked in without anyone realising. Odd really when she's actually been invited. Knowing there is now karaoke, I excuse myself from Raphael, who eyes me warily. I head over to the DJ, but I'm stopped in my tracks.

"Let's dance," Lawrence says behind me making me jump. Before I can react, he grabs my hand and leads me to the dance floor. A group of females swamp us and another growl puts them in their place. They slink away but watch from a distance. Lawrence and I start to dance around to the beat of "Tongue Tied" by Grouplove. We bump and grind with

Lawrence taking extra care not to actually touch me apart from the occasional handhold. The song finishes, and "Treasure" by Bruno Mars comes on next. By the time the song is finished, I'm pretty beat, but Lawrence is still full of beans. Of course, he is.

"Just one more dance," he pleads.

"You've had your lot," I say breathlessly.

"Go on," he tries to coax me.

"No more, you fiend," I joke as I walk away and head to over to the DJ. I take a piece of paper and write my request down. Handing it to the DJ, he nods. I can't even try to whisper what I want to sing. Raphael will hear, and I want it to be a surprise. When I head back to where I left Raphael, he's not there, Alex is there, instead. I scan the room and see he's in deep conversation with Lawrence and Evangeline. With him so distracted, I turn my attention back to Alex, who has an impressed but obviously horny look on his face.

"You can stop drooling now." I laugh as I reach him.

"How can I stop drooling after that performance? I'd certainly like to dance with you," he says with a cheeky glint in his eyes and a hand held out to me. Just as I'm about to take it, a growl stops me. Alex's face takes on a lighter shade and his hand drops. I watch as he retreats over to Cindy. A pair of hands grabs my waist and turns me. Raphael is glaring in Alex's direction. His eyes are so intense it scares me. Whoa, what is up with him? I go to pull him up on it, but I think better of it. "Fancy a dance?" I smile at him. I'm beat, but I could happily have one dance with Raphael.

"I do not dance," he says in a low, rich voice. I step back from him in surprise. My eyes rake him up and down.

"How can you not dance?" I ask incredulously. "I know just how good you can move," I say. His eyes turn instantly almost black, and he goes to grab me. My name being called over the speakers interrupts him. I sweetly smile at him, and his face takes on confusion as I turn and head to the DJ.

He hands me a microphone and one of my favourite songs starts to play. Closing my eyes, I start to sing.

CHAPTER TWENTY-FIVE

Raphael

From the moment I saw Rosannah in her black dress, I have wanted nothing more than to get her out of it. Unfortunately, we had to come to this party. I thought it would be a little affair, but this must be some kind of joke. All the humans with the exception of Rosannah think they have just been to a wedding. Everything here is typical for humans from the DJ playing the usual party songs to the decorations on the tables scattered around the room. With there being free booze, most of the humans are already tipsy.

This party is such a farce that the only Synod members here are Vladimir and me. The others politely excused themselves with fictitious plans that were too important and had been planned for months. Even Reggie showed a rare display of compassion in declining the invitation to this party. You see, the act of a human starting the transition really is something to see, but a party like this is just boring. We know what vampires look like; we see them all the time.

I would not have normally come to something like this, but I am only here so that Rosannah can see how Blondie has transformed from a dying wreck to a *living* vampire. Although she is no longer blond, I will probably always think of her as Blondie, just like Lawrence will always think of her as the Panty Strangler.

166

With Blondie, I do have to admit that I have met many humans in my time, and I did not think it was possible for any of them to be as stupid as she appeared to be. Thankfully, it was all an act. How I did not see through it is beyond me. It probably has to do with the fact that I think humanity is ridiculous, and I do not have much faith in humans. They are incredibly stupid, and amazingly, they are crueller, greedier, and more thoughtless than we are. At least most of us vampires do not make them suffer, much. I am sure I can speak for most of us. Believe me, I have met all of our kind here on this Earth. When I say that we do not take land or property, and we do not kill to get our hands on a feeble old relative's inheritance, I mean we do not stomp on others on our journey to the top.

We achieve the things we want through hard work. There is a buried sense of pride in our kind that may sit below the surface but comes to play when we set our sights on something. We happily work tirelessly; maybe one day the human race will learn something from us, but I doubt it. It appears to be an inbred thing. A human has self-respect and pride, or they do not. We are not the noblest of creatures; we drink blood, but even then, there are ways and means to get this without the unnecessary harming of any living creature. Now, do not think of me as a hypocrite. I do enjoy tormenting humans without caring about their regard. I do get a large kick out of it, but humans are certainly not innocent, naïve little beings. They know exactly what they are doing. Like this Alex.

He is talking to Rosannah, and I have to fight the rage I feel not to rip him apart. He may be a lost sheep in a herd-less flock, but any fool can see his attraction to Rosannah. He plays on this, and to me, this is a very dangerous thing. I make my way over to them, interrupting their little conversation by slipping between them, and wrap an arm around Rosannah's waist. This is human body talk for *she is mine*. As opposed to vampire body language where I would growl and then throw the offender across the room. This is reserved for normal vampires. The Synod is a different matter, but I've slammed Reggie into many a wall over the time I have known him. I am quite glad when Lawrence turns up, but before I can get to him, he turns on the showman that resides inside and plays up for all the ladies, including Rosannah.

Once they have finished their dance, I grab Lawrence and whisk him into a corner. I am appalled by the amount of excuses for females that growl at *me,* but one death glare has them scattering away.

"What the hell is he doing here?" I growl at him as Evangeline joins us.

"Who?" Lawrence asks, oblivious to the pathetic excuse for a life he was meant to be keeping an eye on that is parading around here.

"Alex," I growl.

"Oh yeah, him. He's talking to Rosannah as we speak," he says with a smile.

"Again?" I ask in disbelief.

"What's the problem?" Lawrence asks with a knowing grin.

"Yeah, what is the problem, Raphael?" Evangeline pipes up.

"Apart from the very obvious, you were meant to be keeping an eye on him. Why is he here?" I ask, ignoring Evangeline, who pouts at my rudeness.

"Well, Raphael, he is family. To the Panty Strangler, that is," he says with a snigger.

"What? Actually, never mind. Why did you not tell me that he was coming here?" I ask him.

"I can't keep an eye on him twenty-four seven and keep you up-to-date on his every move. I do have a life you know!" he says with annoyance.

"Really? This is news to me. I have always been under the impression that you are a nobody," I say deadpan.

"Ow," he says with feigned hurt.

"Do I have to get Evangeline to babysit you again?" I ask. A look of horror appears on his face.

"There is no way I am teaming up with him again," Evangeline shoots at me as she whisks off to speak to Blondie. Lawrence then places his hands on my shoulders.

"Raphael, the real problem here isn't me, it's Alex. He isn't a threat to your relationship. Rosannah loves you and wouldn't leave you for anything in the whole entire world. Look at you. You're a hot piece of vampire ass..."

"Please stop before I throw up," I interrupt him.

"Look, all I'm trying to say is that you don't have to be jealous." He grins at me.

"Are you a complete moron? Has it slipped your mind that he tried to *rescue* her and that a vampire we are yet to identify is pulling his wretched strings in an attempt to get to her?" I ask him.

"Yes, but she still loves only you," he says as I turn from him.

"Idiot," I mutter as I head back over to Rosannah.

After chasing that thing away from Rosannah, I am left high and dry by her. I watch as she makes her way over to the DJ.

"Raphael," a familiar yet toned down voice says beside me. I turn to see the smiling face of Blondie.

"What a party. It really is something else," I say. She smiles as a piano piece starts through the speakers.

"Isn't it just. I'm so glad you both came." She smiles at me. I must admit the dark hair seems to suit her, but it does seem a bit dramatic. Just then, the most beautiful sound hits me. The most heavenly singing caresses and soothes my ears. There are gasps all around, and I turn in stunned surprise to see the voice of an angel belongs to Rosannah. With her eyes closed tight, she stands there singing her heart out to one of my favourite songs, "Songbird." I am not one for sentimental crap, as you know, but this song has always struck a chord within me. I am vaguely aware of high-pitched squeaks nearby. I stand transfixed the whole time Rosannah is singing. When she finishes, the whole room is in stunned silence. It is broken when Blondie rushes over to Rosannah and the place erupts with cheers. Once everyone calms down, Rosannah sheepishly makes her way over to me.

"That was..." I leave the words hanging in the air. Nothing I can say will be enough to describe what I have just heard. Rosannah's face screws up a little, and I can tell something is bothering her. Pleased for the unintentional break she has given me; I latch onto it. "What is wrong?" I whisper as I take her into my arms.

"Cindy," she whispers back. I look at Blondie, who looks over at us. Of course, she can hear us, she is a vampire now, but before I can warn Rosannah of this, she continues. "Her crying without any tears is just so strange. I still haven't gotten over Evangeline crying with laughter and no actual tears coming out." She continues to whisper, and Blondie is smiling in amusement. I smile back, but the smile does not last long. I can convey emotion like any other creature can, but I will never be able to cry tears for Rosannah. The inability to cry has not bothered me for some years, but it bothers me a little now. Rosannah pulls back and looks up at me. I force a smile at her, and she snuggles into our hug.

CHAPTER TWENTY-SIX

Rosannah

"I need to visit the little girl's room," I say pulling back from our hug. Raphael growls lightly but lets me go. I head out of the hall, and I realise that I have no idea where the toilet actually is. I walk up to the butler who is humming a tune to himself. "Excuse me?" I ask.

"Yes?" he replies.

"I was wondering where the toilet was," I say sheepishly.

"It's just up the stairs, first door on the left." He smiles.

I race up there and do my business. I'm amazed at the size and splendour of the bathroom, but I want to get back to the party. Once I've washed my hands, I leave the bathroom. The sight of Alex makes me jump.

"Oh, my goodness. You startled me," I say breathlessly.

"Is he your boyfriend?" Alex asks. I have no idea if he is or not, but I'm not going to tell Alex that he's not.

"You could say that," I say.

"Are you fucking him?" he asks.

"Excuse me?" I ask.

"I asked you if you're fucking him," he says.

"That is none of your business," I say.

"I'm just trying to figure out why you're not interested in me," he says.

"I've told you before. You're a nice guy, but you're not what I'm looking for," I say. A low rumble sounds out from nearby. This is bad; this is very bad. I turn and see Raphael making his way over to us. He fixes Alex in a glare and wraps an arm around me.

"We are leaving, now," he whispers in my ear. Any other time, I would protest, but right now, it's the best idea I've probably ever heard. Without saying a word, we walk off leaving Alex standing there.

"I should say goodbye to Cindy and Vladimir," I say.

"I have already done that for both of us," he says as we make our way to his car.

Raphael opens the door and waits until I'm sat before he closes the door and races off. With a giant leap, he clears the trees that border the drive. Within seconds, I hear a large roar and an incredible cracking sound. A loud bang then a low rumble follows. After a few moments, Raphael comes back clearing the trees and is instantly in the car.

"Do your seatbelt up," he says. I do as I'm told as Raphael starts the car up. He turns around and races off.

"Want to talk about what just happened?" I ask.

"No," he says simply with a tight grip on the steering wheel.

We spend a majority of the journey in silence as we head back home. Home; that's an interesting word. I have my home with Marmalade, but I also think of the room that was my prison in Raphael's house as home.

"Are you glad you came?" Raphael asks pulling me from my thoughts. Ah, so we can't talk about what happened with Alex or what he did when he ran off, but we can talk about other things?

"I think you know the answer to that." I laugh.

"I just want to make sure that you are okay with all of this now," he says, eyes dead ahead.

"Yes, I'm all okay now. It's the whole *dying* part I'm not all right with, though. I know it's part of the process, but I don't like it. It's quite traumatic," I say fiddling with my thumbs.

"But did she not look much better?" he asks. I'm not too sure what road he's heading down with this or why he hasn't used Cindy's name. My mind goes into overload. Could he possibly think females look better if they're vampires? That I'd look better as a vampire? Maybe he's just referring to Cindy. She was in a very bad way when she was *dying*, and that's a good way of putting it, and now she looks amazing.

"Yeah, she did," I say with a half-hearted smile.

"You see that she is fine now," he says with a satisfied smile.

"She's a vampire. I don't know if she can be classified as fine now," I say looking out of the window into the blackness. I know that with his vampire eyes, he can see more than I ever could out there, but I would rather not look at him right now. I feel slightly annoyed but mainly embarrassed.

"You do not like what I am." It's a statement, not a question.

"Yes, no. I mean, it's the changing I don't like," I say, my voice small. He pulls up, and I wonder what's going on when I realise we're outside my apartment. I hadn't noticed the change from pitch black to civilisation.

"You do not like vampires," Raphael says a little more sternly.

"Well, from what I've seen so far, they're not the noblest creatures," I say.

"Noble! What the hell would you know about us? You have known us for five minutes, and now you act like you know everything about us!" He explodes at me. In a blind panic, I get out of the car and race up to my flat. I rummage for what seems like forever in my handbag trying to find my keys. Once I grab them, my hands shake so much they jump from one palm to the other as I try to locate the door key. I curse the fact that the four keys on the ring have turned into a million in my clumsy fumble. Eventually, I grab the right key, get into my apartment, and lock the door behind me. Raphael hasn't followed me, and I hear a car race off into the distance. I'm so confused. Why would it bother him that I think vampires aren't saints? He knows this!

Feeling disheartened, I say hi to Marmalade. I feed her and then have a shower. Once I'm dried and in my pjs, I come into the front room intent on bolting the front door. Now that I've calmed down a little, I remember that I didn't do it. The sight of Raphael sat on the couch with Marmalade in his lap stops me. After an initial yelp of fright, wonder and awe overcomeme.

"How..." I can't formulate the question. Raphael moves Marmalade to the side, who protests with a slight hiss, and stands in front of me in the blink of an eye.

"I have a key," he states as if it's nothing.

"But you drove off!" I exclaim.

"I ran back," he says.

"But, wait, you have a key?" I ask incredulously.

"I had all your keys cut a while back," he says looking down at Marmalade, who's now weaving her way around his ankles. *Traitor.* I'm not sure if I'm angry, happy, or freaked out. This means he could have entered my flat whenever he wanted to over the past month and a half. That morning that I was sure my answering machine was full and then mysteriously was empty by the time I came home from work. He must have erased them. I look down at Marmalade, who's happily purring at him. I don't know what to think, but anger wins over.

"I'm going to bed, and I want you gone," I state as I walk off to my room. I close the door and lean against it. A shove of the door and I go sprawling across the bed. I flip over to see a very intimidating Raphael filling the doorway. His eyes are jet black and anger is dripping off him like water if he were soaked.

"I have told you before. You will not walk away from me!" he yells at me.

"I can and I will," I say jumping up from the bed. My bravery will only allow me to shout at him but not get close. It's stupid really because he can get to me before I can blink.

"No, you will not," he growls at me. My heart is breaking once again, but sense is talking to me through the painful haze of devastation.

"Oh, come on, Raphael, wake up and smell the coffee," I say. He pulls a face of slight distaste, and in a flash, he's at my throat. His fangs pierce the skin and sink into the flesh. I cry out, and the familiar fire burns its way through my body as he sucks. I push at his chest, and he pulls back with a slightly pained expression.

"Now definitely isn't the time to bite me into oblivion," I say breathlessly.

"Bite you into oblivion?" he asks with a smirk.

"That's not the point, but it proves what I've been saying. We are just not compatible. You're a three-hundred-year-old vampire who's been through more than I could ever imagine. You will live forever. You're indestructible, for goodness' sake! You are the most beautiful creature I have ever seen and will probably ever see, and I'm..." I look down at myself.

"Don't," he growls at me.

"I'm nothing. I'll grow old and grotesque and die in no time at all compared to how long you've been around. You should be with your own kind," I say as tears threaten. The truth cuts deep.

"I do not want a vampire or anyone else. You are my everything. You saved me, you saved me!" he yells at me. He is so blinded by stupidity. "You are worried about getting old? I can fix that for you," he says taking a step closer to me.

"Don't you dare!" I scream at him. "Don't you ever offer me that!" I grate at him.

"You really do not ever want to be like me? To live forever?" he asks with a puzzled look.

"I've told you before that I don't want to be like you. Why on earth would I want to be a vampire? It's not just about living forever, is it? It's all the other stuff that comes with it. I may not like certain things about life, but I'm happy as I am," I say. A pained look flashes across Raphael's face, but it's gone before I can really register it. "We're at a stalemate, but it still doesn't change the fact that we just don't fit together," I whisper. In a flash, he has me in his arms, and his hand is down the front of my shorts with his fingers buried deep in me. I gasp at the sudden sensation.

"See how you react to me," he growls as he pulls his fingers out of me. "You're soaking already." He holds up two glistening fingers. I stand there speechless as he strips off his coat, shirt, and shoes. He pulls my vest up over my head and then pushes me back onto the bed before peeling off my shorts and panties. Without saying a word, he drops his face between my legs and licks the apex of my thighs. I shudder and moan as the coolness of his tongue hits my burning flesh. He climbs up on me and looks deep into my eyes. "You see, it is not that I am an incredible lover that has you reacting like this," he says, and his mouth latches onto my left breast.

"Please." I squirm and beg. I need him buried deep inside of me, and if he isn't soon, I'm going to go insane. He lifts his head, and my hard nipple pops out of his mouth.

"It is because it is *me* who is doing this to you," he says and then hops back, lowering his face between my legs. He places his thumb at the top of my folds and pulls them up towards me so that the sensitive bundle of nerves hidden beneath can be seen. He then lowers his mouth to it and massages it slowly with his tongue. He captures me in an intense gaze, and I can't look away as I watch him licking my aching bud. Slowly, he rubs the end of his tongue up and down, over and over. It's sweet, sweet torture, and soon, I feel myself build up to an orgasm. My breathing gets faster and faster.

"Oh God, that feels sooo good," I whimper. He clamps down and sucks hard, pulling the whole bud into his mouth. I scream as I come in his mouth. He rides all the waves out, tonguing my slick, silky slit while I arch my back, and my hands bury themselves in the duvet. Once the last wave has passed, I collapse back onto the bed. Raphael's jeans and boxers are off in a flash, and he is soon on top of me, hovering just above me on his elbows, looking down at me with a glint in his jet black eyes. My legs instinctively wrap around his waist, and I can feel his erection pressing against me.

"You see; this is not normally how the act of sex is. It is because *we* are making love to one another," he says as he slams into me.

"*Ah.*" We both yell in twisted pleasure and emotional pain.

"Do not ever tell me that we do not *fit*," he says through gritted teeth as his hips slap against the backs of my thighs. "Nothing will ever feel as good as *me* inside of *you,*" he hisses as he continues his thrusts. Desperation laces his words. I look into his eyes, and I can see he means every word. "Because we are one," he says with strangled emotion as we come together. He collapses on me, and my heart swells. A sense of calm washes over me and a peaceful serene sits static in the air.

CHAPTER TWENTY-SEVEN

Raphael

I awake to find the bed empty. This is a surprise to me. I must have been in such a deep sleep that I did not notice Rosannah leave the bedroom. I have always been aware of my surroundings during sleep but making love with Rosannah is so emotionally draining. Draining in a really great way, of course, but it can sometimes put me into a deep sleep. I put my boxers on, and I am in the kitchen at speed. Rosannah is at the sink dressed in tight jeans and a jumper. She has not noticed I am here and lightly hums to herself a song I do not believe I have heard before. The cat appears to approve as she meows tunefully by her feet. Rosannah gives a little bum wiggle here and there, which I find incredibly sexy. Rosannah has the perkiest ass I have ever laid eyes on. She turns around and yelps quite loudly when she spots me.

"I don't think I'll ever get used to you sneaking around," she pants.

"I do not sneak around. I am just much more nimble than most." I smile as I walk over to her. I pull her into my arms and look into her eyes. All I see is happiness, contentment, and a sense of belonging. It saddens me. There is a spark in her eyes that I know will one-day fade. I was against Rosannah going through the transition because in all honesty I

180

respected her feelings on the matter, and although I still respect her decision, I do not like it anymore. It is incredibly selfish of me to hate the fact that Rosannah does not want to be a vampire. Not only would I have her forever, but it would also be much safer. There would be nothing anyone or anything could do to her. I would not have to worry about her getting sick or dying either. Rosannah is so against becoming one of us that it is not even up for discussion, which I also dislike.

Rosannah smiles at me, bringing my attention back to her.

"I have something I'd like to ask you," she says with an underlying tone of caution. I have a feeling I am not going to like what she has to say. "Brianna and Michael are having a special dinner tonight that they have invited me to. I really don't want to be the third wheel. So, I was wondering if you would come along with me?" she asks. Ah, yes. Sack of potatoes. Though Rosannah has mentioned some kind of transformation.

"What is the special occasion?" I ask.

"They declared their undying love for one another." She sighs.

"This is for real?" I ask. Rosannah giggles lightly and nods. "Then we have missed an important event in our relationship. We declared our undying love for one another and did not announce it to the world. We have failed at the first hurdle," I say with a smirk. Rosannah bursts out laughing then her face drops.

"We have a relationship?" she asks with knitted brows.

"I know you, and you know me," I smirk. I am only playing with her, but she looks a little disappointed. "We love each other, and we are exclusive, are we not?" I ask her.

"Yeah," she whispers.

"Then I suppose we are boyfriend and girlfriend." I smile.

"I've never had a boyfriend before." Rosannah frowns.

"You do not need to feel left out because neither have I." I smile, and Rosannah giggles. I love the sound of her laughter and wait for her to stop before I give her my answer. "I shall go to this farce of a celebration dinner, but only because you want me there," I say. Rosannah smiles and plants a chaste kiss on my lips.

"There's just one more thing I should I tell you. Brianna's boyfriend really looks like Nicholas. I mean *really* looks like him," she says. This has me intrigued. Now I know why she queried with Lawrence what had happened to Nicholas. She wanted to be sure that Brianna's boyfriend definitely was not him. I am very certain Nicholas is still in Chile, but I will find out for sure later on.

Later that evening, we are walking into a French restaurant. Looking across the room, I see a redhead waving enthusiastically at Rosannah. This surely cannot be a sack of potatoes? I stare slightly bewildered at her until her eyes meet mine. She openly gawks at me, and I feel somewhat embarrassed. This is not normal for me, but Rosannah has changed many things within me, and anyone's eyes other than Rosannah's undressing me does not sit right with me anymore. Suddenly, a face that can only be described as looking like an overdone leather dolly appears in front of me. It is immensely offensive.

"Can I help you at all?" she asks revealing hideous yellow teeth. "With *anything*?" she adds and tries to tempt me by waving a pair of saggy and over tanned breasts at me. If I had a normal stomach, then I am sure I would throw up a little in my mouth.

"Leave me alone and do not bother me again," I quietly growl at her. A look of horror spreads across her face, but she moves to the side and lets us pass. I look at Rosannah, who appears to be trying to kill the woman with a mere look. Holding her hand, I lead her to the table where her friend is sitting. There is a man sat facing away from us, but I can instantly tell something is amiss with him. The closer we get the more certain I am of it. The man is a vampire. There is only one heartbeat coming from the table, and it is not his. I pray to God that he is not Nicholas. As we approach, the man turns around, and I feel like I have been knocked over. Female voices fade into the distance as I stare at the face in front of me. There is no doubt that he is Nicholas. Everyone apart from me is completely oblivious. Of course, they would be; their human ears could not deduce that his heart does not beat.

"Raphael, I said how amazing does Brianna look," Rosannah says. I pull my attention away from my brother to look at the sack of potatoes. It is a complete transformation, and she deserves the dignity of being referred to by her name.But I cannot get my mind around the fact that not only has my brother, who is meant to be in Chile undergoing therapy, is sat right in front of me, but he has alsocompletely fooledRosannah and Brianna.

Brianna hops up and sits next to Nicholas leaving a long seat for Rosannah and me to sit on. Rosannah slides in first and I after her.

"Brianna, Michael, this is my boyfriend, Raphael," Rosannah says as Brianna makes an excited squeaking sound. "And this is Brianna, who I've told you a lot about, and this is her boyfriend, Michael." She smiles gesturing to Nicholas. What the hell is he playing at? Lawrence must know about this; he has some serious explaining to do.

Nicholas holds out his hand for me to shake. I take it, and I am not surprised when he uses his full vampire strength to grip my hand. It does not hurt at all, but it has an unsaid insult hidden behind it. I shoot him a glare, and his lip curls up in a snide smile. A waitress comes over, and I am horrified to see it is the *lady* who greeted us. She sheepishly takes orders from everyone and comes to me last.

"And what can I get for you, sir?" she asks. She is wise to speak to me the way she should have the last time we spoke.

"I am fine. Thank you," I say as she retreats from our table as fast as she can.

"Are you sure you don't want anything? It will be weird if we're all eating, and you're not," Brianna says.

"I am not hungry at all and do not want to eat or drink," I say as I brainwash her into dropping the subject. Nicholas leans over to her and whispers in her ear.

"Ask him why," he orders her. Rosannah does not hear this, of course.

"Why aren't you hungry?" she asks me.

"It seems that something," I look over at Nicholas, "has really turned my stomach, and I do not want to risk eating anything. I am here out of politeness," I say flicking my eyes back to Brianna.

"Aw, poor you. If you have to go, just go. It's not a problem at all." She smiles at me.

"Thank you for being so understanding." I smile back. It is my turn to smirk at Nicholas. When I look at Rosannah, she is confused. I half smile at her, but it does not wash. She knows something is bothering me, but she does not say anything about it.

The rest of the dinner is very unpleasant. Rosannah and Brianna have no idea that Michael is really Nicholas. I have to watch as he eats, drinks, and pulls Brianna in close for kisses every now and then all the while throwing smirks and snide looks at me. He is cutting this incredibly fine. He eventually gets up and heads over to the till to pay for the entire meal that he has insisted on paying. I follow him over, and before I can question him, a guy appears. Once Nicholas has paid the bill and the guy has disappeared, I am straight at him.

"What the hell are you playing at, Nicholas?" I ask him.

"I have no idea who this Nicholas is. I am Michael," he says with feigned surprise.

"Cut it out. You know it is impossible for you to trick me," I growl at him.

"Oh, now that you mention it, I may know this Nicholas you speak of." He laughs.

"Answer me. What are you up to?" I demand.

"Now that would spoil things, wouldn't it, brother?" he asks.

"What has gotten into you?" I ask.

"Oh, come on, Raphael. You know exactly what has gotten into me." He smiles.

"Tell me what you are up to," I beg.

"Never mind what I am up to. Just know that I spend a lot of my time balls deep in her best friend," he sneers at me.

"Why her best friend?" I ask.

"Isn't it obvious? She was second best. Now I am always there, always hanging around. I have wormed my way into being a permanent fixture in Rosannah's life, and she has no idea. I mean, she did at first, but I sorted those pesky worries out very quickly." He grins.

"If you harm either of them..." I start.

"You'll what? Kill me? I don't think so. Neither you nor The Synod can do anything because I'm not breaking any rules. I will continue to play for as long as I see fit," he says with an underlying tone. Nicholas and I have had our fair share of disagreements; we have done things from shouting at each other to throwing each other off buildings, but we have never been so wickedly nasty to one another.

"I do not know what has happened to my brother, but you are not him," I say with deepening sadness.

"The brother you knew and loved has gone. He was killed off. For that, my dear Raphael, you are a murderer," he says with gritted teeth.

"No, Nicholas, you are just lost. You see, Lawrence and I have a place within the family, within society, but you? You are the lost brother," I say as I make my way back to Rosannah.

CHAPTER TWENTY-EIGHT

Rosannah

Everything was fine until we walked into the restaurant. I mean I've had my fair share of ups and downs, but I thought it was all behind me. I was happy, and I knew I was safe. Now I am unsure. For starters, some nasty looking woman openly tried it on with Raphael as if I wasn't even there. I felt great pride when he told her to go do one. I thought the evening would be okay after that little glitch, but I had no idea what was to transpire.

Raphael and Michael had been funny all evening. The testosterone levels were through the roof, and for some strange reason, Brianna didn't appear to notice. I don't even know if Raphael has any hormones. Probably not but wouldn't a man have a serious struggle to perform if they had low testosterone? Well, Raphael certainly has no trouble performing, that's for sure.

Once we had all finished eating, Michael insisted on paying the bill. I thought Raphael was just being polite when he followed him to the till. You know, offer to pay half or some towards it, but I was surprised to see that once the bill was paid for, they started having some kind of disagreement. Brianna appeared none the wiser, but everyone else in the restaurant could see that something wasn't right. After a few minutes, Raphael came storming back over to me while Michael followed with a smarmy smirk on his face. What the hell was going on?

"We have to go," Raphael said with tight lips. Something definitely wasn't right.

"What's wrong?" I asked him getting up from my seat. His eyes flicked to Brianna's and a look of worry befell his face. He didn't want to explain it in front of her.

"I will tell you about it later," he said with regret. Michael walked up to Raphael and clapped a hand on his shoulder.

"Oh Raphael, it's fine to explain it now." He smiled. "Brianna, go and freshen up in the little girls' room. I'll send Rosannah to collect you," he ordered her. Brianna smiled widely and trotted off to the ladies'. That was not the Brianna I knew. She was belittled by a man and happily took it. She would never stand for that! Michael watched as her go and once the door to the ladies' closed, he turned his stare to me. "Go ahead, Raphael. Explain," he said without looking away from me. Raphael sighed, bringing my attention to him.

"Michael is Nicholas," he said gauging my reaction. I felt like I had been hit by a ton of bricks and then some. I was so convinced in the beginning that he was Nicholas, but he managed to change my mind with his human traits. How he managed, it didn't matter at that moment. I looked at him in horror.

"You, you're Nicholas? I bloody knew it!" I said pointing a finger at him.

"Yes, I know. Quite the act, huh?" he said with a sneer.

"How could you do this to Brianna?" I asked incredulously.

"Very easily. She's been heavily brainwashed." He grinned. The grin instantly reminded me of Lawrence. What went so wrong with Nicholas? Hello, he's a bloody vampire!

"But she loves you unless that's been stamped into her brain, too," I said.

"Oh, she did that all on her own," he said continuing to grin as if it's an achievement. I suppose it is but not like that!

"But what about all the things you two have done?" I asked.

"Ah well you see, some of those were implanted," he said, the grin finally dropping off his face. It could be that he felt ashamed of what he'd done, but it was more as if he was embarrassed he hadn't achieved all of the things Brianna had boasted about.

"You what?" I asked him, taking a step towards him, but Raphael put an arm around my waist and stopped me from moving any closer to Nicholas. His eyes darted down and laughed, unimpressed at Raphael's gesture.

"At first, I didn't know how to approach her," he said as his eyes returned to mine. "Just looking at her, I couldn't bring myself to make any actual memories with her straight away. So I brainwashed her into coming back to my place and made up a first encounter I thought would be a satisfactory story to tell you and her family," he said with a shrug like it was nothing. I was beyond disgusted.

"What else did you implant in her head?" I asked not wanting to really know, but I had to know what else he'd done to my best friend.

"Most of our encounters, in the beginning, were fabricated. I couldn't bear to touch her until I got her sorted out. That's when I came up with the idea of the holiday. We spent a week in Wales with her not eating much and exercising while I enjoyed myself. Once she shed that weight and sorted her hair out, I was then happy to stick my dick in her," he said.

"You bastard!" I yelled as I tried to lunge at him. Raphael gripped me tighter but growled at Nicholas.

"Raphael, get your woman under control. Oh, that's right, you can't, can you!" He laughed.

"He doesn't need to control me to get me to be his girlfriend," I spat at him. The look fell off his face, and Raphael chuckled lightly.

"Well, now she's in love with me, so something worked," Nicholas said.

"You won't get away with this. I won't let it continue," I said through gritted teeth. I must have gotten to him because he was taken aback, but his face hardened a little, and he leant forward.

"You can try that if you like, but I have her brainwashed into killing herself if anyone intervenes," he said.

"I don't believe you," I said, crossing my arms, hoping to call his bluff. Nicholas straightened back up.

"You can test it out if you want, but if she's your best friend, I wouldn't risk it if I were you," he said with a frown.

"The Synod will hear about this," I told him.

191

"There is nothing they can do. He has not broken any laws," Raphael whispered to me. I turned and glared at him. He rubbed my back as if trying to convey an unspoken message. I sighed and slumped my shoulders.

"I think we're done here. You can go and get Brianna now," Nicholas ordered. I headed off to the ladies'. Brianna was just standing staring at herself in the mirror as if in a daze.

"You can come back now," I told her. No reaction. *You have to be kidding me.*

"*Michael* wants you back now," I almost growled at her. Life returned to her eyes, and she turned to face me with a huge smile. Without saying a word, she headed back out to Nicholas. I followed and saw that the tension between Raphael and Nicholas appeared to have calmed down a little. As Brianna got to Nicholas, she hugged and kissed him.

"Isn't he just amazing? I love him so much," she gushed. I nearly threw up on her shoes.

"We have to get going. I'll see you at work," I said and pulled Raphael by the hand out of the restaurant.

By the time we got to my place, I was a wreck. I couldn't stop the tears from falling.

"What the hell is wrong with him?" I asked Raphael.

"I do not know. I have never seen him like this," he replied. "How long have they been going out together?" he asked me.

"A few months," I sobbed. "Do you think Brianna is in any danger?" I asked him.

"Going by what Nicholas said, Brianna will be safe as long as no one intervenes. I will sort this all out,

but I need to go now. I will be back as soon as I can,"
Raphael said soothingly. Before I could say anything,
he was gone. I'm now sat on the couch as Marmalade
snuggles on my lap as I cry my eyes out wondering
about me and my friend's safety.

CHAPTER TWENTY-NINE

Raphael

I told Rosannah what she needed to hear. I race back home not knowing how to actually sort this out, but I know what will make me feel a little better. I am glad to see the gates are open when I arrive, indicating the others are here. I burst through my front door.

"Hey, Raph," says Lawrence as I walk towards him. Without a word, I punch him straight in the face. His solid face is light against my equally solid fist, and the force sends him flying back into the kitchen. It causes him no damage, but he collides with my breakfast bar, destroying it. He is standing before the last remnants of dust have settled on the floor. A look of utter shock has taken over his features.

"What the hell, Raph!" he exclaims as I grab him by the throat. Evangeline appears and tries to pry my hand off Lawrence.

"How dare you not tell me!" I roar at him.

"What are you talking about?" he screams at me.

"Where is Nicholas?"

"Oh, for God's sake, put him down, Raphael," says Evangeline. I drop him, and he straightens himself out.

"You know where he is. He's in Chile," he says.

"Try again," I growl at him.

"Raphael, I don't know what you're trying to get at, but Nicholas is in Chile," he says.

"Oh, I shall explain it to you, and maybe something will sound familiar and jog your memory. A couple of days after you came back—leaving our dear brother in Chile—he left. He then came back, brainwashed Rosannah's best friend into a relationship, and has been parading around as her human boyfriend ever since!" I yell at him.

"Impossible. I would have known if he had left Chile," he says.

"That is exactly what I am thinking!" I yell at him.

"I swear to you, Raphael. I had no idea. They promised me that they would tell me if he tried to leave! You have to believe me," he begs.

"You knew he loved her and did not tell me about that. You were in cahoots with him to help him try it on with her. Why on earth should I believe you?" I ask him.

"I told you before that I knew he liked her but not loved her, and I thought he just wanted to dance with her. He played it off as another bet. I didn't know he would go all crazy!" he says.

"How can I trust you now?" I ask throwing my arms up in the air.

"Raphael, I haven't lied to you, and I can't tell you about the things I don't know. I haven't done anything wrong here!" he yells at me. My anger is beginning to abate, and I am starting to see sense.

"I suppose you are right. I am sorry, Lawrence. This whole situation is very unsettling," I say. Lawrence places a hand on my shoulder.

"It's all right, Raphael. You're hurting. We all are. Do you know where Nicholas is now?" he asks me.

"I do not personally, but I am sure Rosannah knows. However, she is not in a fit state to ask at this moment in time," I say. Evangeline gasps.

"Goddamn him!" Lawrence yells. I easily forget that Lawrence and Evangeline care about Rosannah and worry for her welfare almost as much I do. "I'm going to phone those vampires in Chile to find out what the hell went wrong," Lawrence says as he pulls out his mobile phone. He punches in a number, and we all stand there as it rings. He holds it against his ear. There is no need to put it on the loudspeaker; we can easily hear the conversation that follows.

"Hello, Chile V Retreat. I'm Louisa, how can I help you?" a sickly sweet voice says. She is clearly human. I can hear her breathing and heartbeat.

"This is Lawrence Monstrum, and I want to know why my brother, Nicholas Monstrum, is no longer there," he asks.

"I am sorry. I cannot divulge patient information," she says regretfully.

"Well, our older brother is a member of The Synod. And considering that the patient has gone on a brainwashing spree and is putting humans at risk, I suggest you start talking," Lawrence threatens.

"Every vampire claims the same thing. You're no different," she says and hangs up. As Lawrence launches into a rage full of profanities, I send a quick text to Mathias and within minutes, Lawrence's phone rings.

"Hello?" He answers.

"I am terribly sorry. What do you need to know?" the sickly sweet voice asks.

"You can start by telling me why my brother left?" Lawrence asks.

"His record states he discharged himself," she says.

"How could you let him leave?" he asks.

"This service is completely voluntary. We cannot force vampires to stay against their will," she says.

"I left specific instructions that I was to be notified if he tried to leave. The receptionist promised me!" he yells down the phone.

"I'm very sorry, but it's against our policy to do that. No vampire can be a legal guardian of another, and because of that, no one can be in charge of their care. The receptionist you would have spoken to would have known that," she says.

"I would like to speak to her now," Lawrence demands.

"I am afraid she has since left," she says, her voice wavering.

"This is not good enough. If anything bad happens as a result of this, you will be hearing from us very soon," he says and hangs up. "Sorry, Raphael, I had no idea any of this had happened."

"It is okay, Lawrence," I say with an understanding smile. It is not his fault at all. I was trying to place blame where I could do something about it. I should not have taken it out on him.

"What did you do to get her to call back?" asks Evangeline pulling me back from my thoughts.

"I texted Mathias," I say with a shrug.

"What did you say?" she asks with surprise.

"I just told him that we were trying to see how Nicholas's treatment was going in Chile, but they would not tell us anything. Looks like he phoned and gave them a piece of his mind." I shrug. "I am going to head back to Rosannah."

CHAPTER THIRTY

Rosannah

I have no idea how long I've been crying, but a knock on the door stops me. I open the door to let Raphael in. He shuts and locks the front door, and he immediately takes me into his arms. I feel lost and cold inside, but our tight embrace warms me back up and makes me feel whole again. When Raphael pulls back from me, he looks at me with slight pity, and it sets me off again. If I'm honest with myself, then I'm not actually sure what upset me. I don't know if it's what happened to my best friend, who is actually pretty happy living a lie she doesn't know she's living, or the fact that my boyfriend's brother has done this. Who am I upset for, Brianna or me?

"Shh," Raphael soothes as his hands rub my back as the tears flow. Raphael is so tender, and his intentions are to calm me down, but I start to get turned on. It really isn't appropriate, but I can't help it. Raphael must pick up on it because his rubs become harder. I gasp as his hands work their way up to my neck. He grunts a reply and grinds his erection into me. I don't know if we can touch each other without the spark of arousal. I push away from him, peel my jumper off over my head, and wriggle out of my jeans to reveal my underwear. Raphael's growl lets me know he approves. Looking at the bulge in his jeans, my mouth starts to salivate. I can't explain why, but I want him in my mouth. I ache to taste him. His hands are at me in an instant, but I bat them away causing a growl of displeasure from him. I attempt to push him backwards, but he's as solid and heavy as a statue.

"Move," I say simply. He looks at me and frowns, but he allows me to direct him back until he is up against the front room windowsill. My hands have a life of their own as they remove his belt. I then undo his fly, and when I drop to my knees, I take his jeans and boxer briefs with me. A look of clarity overcomes Raphael's features as it dawns on him what my intentions are.

"Rosannah," he says with a slightly menacing tone. Ignoring his warning, I take him in my palms. He's rock hard, but the skin is so smooth and soft. Raphael gasps but composes himself as I look up at him. He looks like he's about to explode from a mixture of fear and excitement. It's bizarre, but the sight of him completely at my mercy is something else. His eyes are jet black. Opening my mouth and leaning forward, I run the middle of my tongue up his length. Raphael shouts a curse and jerks in my hands. The feel of him on my tongue is incredible. I want more. Taking another lick up his shaft, I watch as he practically trembles in front of me. Surely, he has had this done plenty of times before? What a thought to have while doing this! I look up at him as I debate plunging him into my mouth. He seems to sense my dilemma because his demeanour changes.

"Don't," he whispers to me. Smiling up at him, I take him slowly into my mouth.

"Damn it!" He growls as he grips the sill behind him.

"Don't break my windowsill," I warn him. I smile inwardly as I suck on him hard. A light rumble sounds, but I continue to take him in and out of my mouth allowing the shaft to slide up and down along my tongue. Occasionally, I flick my tongue across the tip ripping a gasp from him every time. He looks as if he's in pain, and the more I carry on, the more pain he looks like he's in. It surprisingly isn't long before he tenses up, throws his head back, and comes with a loud cry. As his shaft convulses, nothing else happens. In my confused state, Raphael pulls himself out and pulls me to his chest. He plunges his fangs into my neck, and I moan loudly. Once he's finished, he rests his forehead against mine with his eyes shut tight.

"That was..." Raphael leaves the sentence hanging. Kissing me on the lips, he starts to undress me. Once I'm naked, he carries me to the rug and lays me down. I think he likes this spot. My mind clears a little, and my thoughts return. My eyebrows knit as I frown at him. "What's wrong?" he asks concerned.

"Well, I am no expert, but I'm pretty sure that what I just did to you usually results in fluid," I say in embarrassment. "Did I do it wrong?" I ask.

"Oh, you certainly did not do it wrong. You did it so right that I came in minutes," he says looking a little embarrassed.

"Does that not normally happen?" I ask.

"No, it does not," he says.

"But that doesn't explain why there was no fluid." I frown again.

"Look, it is certainly not you. The only fluids in my body are blood and saliva. I have no need for any other ones," he says.

"Oh," I say as I realise I should have already known this. We have never used condoms, and there's been no talk about getting pregnant. How stupid of me! "Can you get STI's?" I ask.

"No. I simply cannot get ill. It is all part of being indestructible," he says. His eyes drop to my naked body, and his eyes take on a darker shade. "Now for me to return the favour," he says with a half-smile. He lowers himself to the apex of my thighs. With a growl, he plunges his tongue deep into me, causing me to scream. He firmly thrusts in and out of me pulling more moans from me. Soon my muscles are tightening up, and just as I'm about to come, a firm knock on the door freezes me. "Ignore it," Raphael whispers and goes to continue, but the knocking becomes louder and consistent. With a growl and a look of thunder, Raphael races off into my bedroom and comes back with a blanket to cover me up. He then strides to the front door and opens it. An amused Lawrence stands there.

"Hi, Rosannah. Good evening?" he asks with a knowing smile. I have no idea how much he heard, but with the front door opening into a short hallway, he can easily see through to me lying here on the front room rug covered with just a blanket. I'm so embarrassed, and my face feels like it's on fire. "Beetroot red really suits you, Rosannah." Lawrence laughs.

"What the hell do you want?" Raphael asks. "Now *really* is not the time Lawrence!" he yells.

"There's been a new development," he says looking at me with concern. A new development? What is he talking about?

202

"Oh, I see," replies Raphael, all traces of anger gone. He races over and crouches in front of me. "I have to go, but I shall be back later," he says.

"What has developed?" I ask him. A look of worry flashes across his face, but it's gone almost instantly.

"Nothing has developed," he says with a forced smile.

"Lawrence didn't whisper. I heard him. He said there was a new development. What is going on?" I ask.

"I do not want you to worry about it. I will explain it all when I get back, but I must go now," he says.

"You better," I warn him.

"I will be back as soon as I can, so I can finish what I started," he says and leans forward to kiss my lips. Lawrence sniggers and Raphael turns, growling at him, cutting him dead. In a flash, they're both gone, and the door is closed. I sit there stunned for a moment but decide I should get dressed. I jump in the shower, and once I'm dressed, I enter the living room. I get as far as the coffee table before there's a knock at the door. Thinking it's Raphael, I open it without looking through the spy hole. I'm shocked to see that it's a grey-eyed Nicholas.

CHAPTER THIRTY-ONE

Raphael

After leaving Rosannah's, we race back to mine and head into the kitchen. I really had to pull myself away from Rosannah when Lawrence arrived. I heard him approach her door but hoped that he would have the decency to leave when he heard what was going on. I cannot describe just how frustrated I am that I had to leave her on the edge and so exposed …

"I'm sorry I had to interrupt you two," Lawrence says.

"What's going on?" Evangeline says as she pops into the kitchen.

"You are here?" I ask in annoyance.

"What's happened?" She ignores me and asks Lawrence.

"Something new has developed. I had to go and pry Raphael off Rosannah, and he's a little pissy about it," Lawrence says.

"He always seems to get really moody when he doesn't get his rocks off," Evangeline says.

"Can we leave my rocks out of this?" I grate.

"See what I mean?" Evangeline says with raised eyebrows to Lawrence.

"Rosannah sounded like she was well on her way. She has quite a pair of lungs on her. I could hear her all the way down the road. You really must have..."

"Stop right there," I interrupt Lawrence. "Just tell me what this new development is," I growl at him.

"I've been monitoring Alex quite a bit recently," he says.

"Ah, so you have actually been doing what you were meant to be doing?" I ask.

"When I have spare time, I have," he replies.

"Yes, of course. What is the development?" I ask with narrow eyes.

"Alex has had another phone call," he says.

"Hopefully, this will give us something to go on," I say.

"Well, not exactly," he says.

"What do you mean?" I ask.

"The caller stated that they have Alex's next instruction and that they will call back in an hour's time to tell him. This gave me the opportunity to come and get you as I thought you would want to listen in, too," he says.

"Very well. That would be the right decision," I say. Lawrence smiles a cocky grin. "For once," I say knocking the grin off his face.

"Let's get going," he says and makes his way to the door. Evangeline follows him.

"Where do you think you are going?" I ask her.

"I'm coming, too," she says with a smile.

"No, you are not. You are going home, and you keep this to yourself. Mathias is getting fed up with your calls, "I say, and Lawrence and I dash off before she can say anything.

CHAPTER THIRTY-TWO

Rosannah

I stare at Nicholas in disbelief. "Why are you here?" I ask. He laughs but then turns serious.

"I want to explain what the hell I've been doing," he says as he moves towards me. I back up, and he closes the door behind him. He stops, but I go back a few extra steps.

"Explaining is a good thing," I say in encouragement.

"This makes me feel weird," he says with a frown. Makes you feel weird? What about me?

"How about I ask you questions, and you can explain what you want?" I suggest.

"Okay, I can do that." He smiles.

"Why did you leave the vampire therapists?" I start.

"I wasn't insane," he says. Okay, we have different opinions on that one, but I'll leave that there.

"Why did you agree to go there then?" I ask.

"It got Lawrence off my back. Once he found me, he wouldn't leave me alone. I know he meant well, but he was seriously pissing me off. After he had left, I waited a few days before I discharged myself. Those few days allowed me to come up with a plan, "he says with a grim expression.

"Do I want to know anything about this plan?" I ask out loud.

"I had originally planned to kidnap you and make you love me. How pathetic is that?" He laughs. Wow, that's really something.

"What changed?" I ask.

"I saw Brianna," he says. Hope sparks in my chest.

"You liked her?" I ask.

"No," he says looking embarrassed. "I thought that if I became her boyfriend, then I could get to know more about you and then lure you into falling for me, especially with Raphael no longer on the scene. I had to do a lot of groundwork first, though," he says.

"How did you know about Raphael?" I ask with intrigue.

"I found out from Brianna that you had no boyfriend, and after sniffing around at your work, I found out what Raphael had done. I realised The Synod must have had something to do with it, but whoever was responsible inadvertently helped me with my human escapade, "he says. I am suddenly desperate to know how he managed to pretend to be human.

"Speaking of human escapades, how you managed to..." I don't know what word to use.

"Be human?" he asks. I nod in reply.

"Well, I cut my hair, which only served to help me take on a new persona, but I suppose you're wondering about the food. I simply forced and kept the food down until I could get rid of it," he says.

"Of course," I say as it hits me. "You're incredibly strong so why wouldn't you be able to keep food down until you wanted to throw it up?" I ask myself. Nicholas gives me a knowing smile. "But that doesn't explain how you made your eyes brown or have a rosy glow to your skin," I say.

"It's a trick we vampires have up our sleeves. It helps pass us off as human. If we had known about it from the beginning, it would have made our early vampire lives much easier." He laughs.

"Why not use it all the time?" I ask.

"Our grey eyes and pale skin aren't as freaky as they used to be. Plus, we can't be bothered to do it all the time," he says with a shrug.

"So you can have any eye colour you want?" I ask after thinking about this for a moment.

"No, only our original eye colour," he replies.

"And black," I add with a smile. Nicholas's eyes darken a little, and the smile drops from my face. We stand in an awkward silence until I decide to break it.

"Well, now you've been caught out," I say with a nervous laugh.

"That wasn't meant to happen," Nicholas says. How long did he think he would get away with it? Unless he thought Raphael was never coming back to me.

"You do know that Raphael and I are in love, don't you?" I ask with slight caution. Nicholas smiles.

"I can see that," he says.

"It's the only reason we slept together," I say.

"I know," he whispers.

"There's just one more thing I'd like to ask. Well, I don't want to, but I think I should ask," I say. "Was everything that happened with Brianna real?" I ask.

"Most, if not all, things were real from when we came back from Wales," he says with a small smile.

"So you've seen sense?" I ask him.

"You could say that," he says.

"Is this all over now? This plan of yours?" I ask hopefully.

"Oh, it's definitely over. The plan was stupid and futile," he says. I breathe a sigh of relief. "How I ever thought it would work is beyond me. Acting the way I did to Raphael in the restaurant has replayed in my head over and over. Every time it's played, I've felt more and more ridiculous. I've realised I was never in love with you as I thought I was. Plus, Brianna is really starting to grow on me," he says with a small, bashful smile.

"Well, if you want to carry on seeing my best friend, I think you should really tell her your real name, at least," I say.

"Yeah. You're right," he says.

"Maybe I should see if Raphael will change my work back to how it was. I'd love for everything to go back," I say. "Are you going to see your brothers and sister?" I ask him.

"I'm going to see Lawrence. Evangeline can wait, but I'm not going to see Raphael anytime soon. I feel too embarrassed," he says with a sheepish expression.

"You can't hide from him forever," I say gently.

"I know. I'm just not ready to face him yet," he says. We stand in silence for a moment.

"Look, Rosannah. I'm sorry about everything," he says.

"I know. Go and see Lawrence. I bet he's missing you like crazy," I say and push his shoulder. He doesn't budge at all. "Thank you, Rosannah," he says and opens the front door.

"Nicholas?" I call to him. He turns and looks at me. "It's good to have you back," I say. Nicholas gives me a cheeky grin and closes the door behind him when he leaves. I walk over to the couch and slump down onto it with a huge sigh. *Ring.* I really hope it's Raphael this time. I fling the door open.

"Raphael, finally-" I stop mid-sentence. There's someone very familiar stood outside my apartment. I recognise them instantly, but their light grey eyes are very, very new. "Y-you can't p-possibly be a v-vampire," I say with a stutter. They only reply with a smile that has me feeling very uneasy. They are at me in the blink of an eye.Before I know it, they have flung me over their shoulder and are dashing down the stairsat speed, slamming my front door shut behind them.

CHAPTER THIRTY-THREE

Raphael

For a while now, we have staked out in Lawrence's usual spot opposite Alex's house hidden among the shadows and out of sight. I feel like we are wasting time as Alex prattles about his living room.

"The call is late," Lawrence says looking at his watch, and with that sentence, the phone rings. It does not sit right with me, but Alex picks up the receiver.

"Hello?" Alex answers.

"I had another instruction for you, but our plans have changed. The matter now has to be taken into our own hands. You have been very useful, and we think you should be rewarded for what you have done for our cause. You are now back to normal." Says a robotic voice.

"You could never actually do magic. It's amazing what confidence can do to humans," a second distorted voice says down the line.

"You must come and see us now for a reward for all of your hard work. Four chicken maids," the first robotic voice says and then hangs up.

"What the hell does that mean?" Lawrence asks.

"I have no idea, but we have made a new discovery. Before, it sounded like there was only one of them, but now it is confirmed there are at least two," I say to Lawrence.

"I think it's funny they referred to what he's done as hard work," Lawrence says.

"Yes, *hard work* indeed," I say sarcastically.

"It's so annoying that they are using voice distorters. They are obviously worried about being recognised," Lawrence says with concern. Right then, Alex leaves his house and walks off down the road in a daze. Lawrence and I look at each other and then follow him. "That strange sentence must be some kind of special instruction," Lawrence says. Sometimes, my brother displays such intelligence, but the rest of the time, he is a complete imbecile.

"Really?" I ask. "If you had not told me that, then I would not have had a clue," I say with mock seriousness. Lawrence looks unimpressed but laughs.

"How long do we follow him for?" he asks.

"For as long as necessary," I reply.

Alex displays the most peculiar behaviour. Every so often, he will walk over to a building, shake his head, and then continue on his journey. I find this very odd, but we continue to follow him for quite some time. Alex manages to walk for hours, eventually heading out of town and down country lanes. It is now pitch black except for the headlights of the odd passing vehicle. How Alex can see where he is going out here is quite something. If human quirks are anything to go by, then this guy must eat a ton of carrots.

"Why on earth is he walking and not driving?" Lawrence asks. I am just about to tell him to shut up when I think about it. Lawrence has a point. The car is pretty awful, but he does have one. Why *would* he walk all this way when he has a car? The road we are on goes for miles and miles before we hit the next signs of civilisation. A horrible feeling suddenly befalls me. Grabbing Lawrence's arm, I stop him in his tracks.

"Why are we stopping?" asks Lawrence.

"How could I have been so stupid?"

"Do you really want me to answer that?" he asks with a grin.

"Lawrence, this is no time for your crap. We have been had," I say.

"How?"

"Are you really that slow? Actually, I cannot say that when I have been just as stupid as you for once," I say.

"What are you talking about, Raph?" he asks.

"You asked it yourself. Why is he walking and not driving? Look at it all. He is walking out of town, down a road that goes for miles before it hits the next town, when he has a car. It is also pitch black out here. At first, I thought his eyes were really good but teamed up with all this walking and his strange behaviour, it is evident we have been led on a wild goose chase. That odd sentence was a pre-installed instruction that we did not know the meaning. See what you missed by not monitoring him properly! This means that the vampires controlling this clown know we have been monitoring him and when you have and have not been listening in!" I say.

"How can they know that?" Lawrence asks.

"Right now, I really do not care why. All I know is that we have to get back to Rosannah NOW!" I yell. We race off at speed towards her flat.

CHAPTER THIRTY-FOUR

Unknown

When word got around about Rosannah and her inability to be brainwashed, I can tell you that I wasn't the only one who sat up and listened. Raphael thought that Rosannah's little indiscretion would be a secret, but The Synod is not a failsafe for secrets.

There have been all kinds of reactions to Rosannah's news, but only three of us have actually been willing to do anything about it. So far, the plan has involved Alex, but the ideas have been less than desired.

First, we had thought it would be a good idea to brainwash Alex up to his eyeballs with a cock and bull story and send him into Raphael's house. Rosannah hated vampires, and a handsome man coming to her rescue looked like a done deal. Little did we know that she harboured feelings for him and would refuse to leave. It was due to my insistence on removing memories of us and our plans from Alex's mind that stopped Raphael from being able to brainwash the truth out of him. All that time and effort put in and all we managed to get out of it was Raphael upping his security.

Once he removed himself from Rosannah's life, it gave us another opportunity. We sent Alex in once again. Raphael had brainwashed him to forget all about Rosannah, but Rosannah had no idea. We played upon this and brainwashed Alex into hanging out at the café where she ate lunch. We even had him sit at her usual table. We had him all set to ask her on a date but remain oblivious to who she actually was. It was only a matter of time before they came across each other. Our plan almost failed, but fortunately, her friend came to our rescue. The first date went well, but we couldn't wait for the next one. We sent him over sooner, but Rosannah wouldn't take a bite of Alex's apple. No matter how tasty and juicy he made it out to be. Once again, we had put in a lot of time and effort but to no avail.

We sent him to his cousin's *wedding reception* with pre-installed instructions, but again, we didn't succeed.

We sat and poured over our failures until the obvious slammed into my brain. If we wanted Rosannah, then we would have to just take her while Raphael was distracted. This is what is currently happening, and it won't be long until Rosannah is no longer a problem.

I look up and start. "Just because you can creep around doesn't mean that you should!" I yell at the individual who has just broken me from my thoughts.

"Sorry," they reply. They appear genuine.

"You are very late," I say.

"I had to deviate from the plan, "they say sheepishly

"You had to WHAT?!" I yell as I rise from my seat.

They recoil at my temper and I calm down a little. It is then that I look down. I have obliterated the armrests of my chair. "Ah," I exclaim. "Please tell me you have her."

"Yes, she's where you told me to put her," they say.

"Well, what are we waiting for? Let's get this show on the road," I say as I dash off.

It takes us minutes to get there, and I can hear Rosannah's sobs as I approach the building. It pleases me that we have a plan that has finally worked, but we won't have much time. Raphael is probably already aware that Alex has led him on a wild goose chase.

I enter the room Rosannah is in and wait until she looks at me. Her eyes widen as she recognises me.

"You," she whispers.

ABOUT THE AUTHOR

Taniquelle Tulipano is an adult romance author who resides in London, England with her husband and daughter.

For updates and to find out more visit:
www.taniquelletulipano.com
www.facebook.com/taniquelletulipano

BOOKS BY TANIQUELLE TULIPANO

The Monstrum Vampire Series

Dead Beginnings (Monstrum #1)
The Lost Brother (Monstrum #2)
Princess of the Dark (Monstrum #3)